BLUE
MOON

BLUE MOON

DALE DAPKINS

ABSOLUTELY AMA⚡ING eBOOKS

ABSOLUTELY AMAZING eBOOKS

Published by Whiz Bang LLC, 926 Truman Avenue, Key West, Florida 33040, USA.

For information contact:
Publisher@AbsolutelyAmazingEbooks.com

ISBN-13: 978-1945772276 (Absolutely Amazing Ebooks)
ISBN-10: 1945772271

**Other Absolutely Amazing eBooks
by Dale Dapkins**

Prize Winners

Prize Winner Stew with Small Dogs

The Art Thief

Ebola

BLUE
MOON

"Every event, no matter how small or large, has a chronological site on a backward scrolling time spiral, each event having been caused by the event previous, and that previous event the product of the one before it, etc. etc. If one journeys backward far enough on the event-time line of living beings, one arrives at the beginning; at the first spark of life ... the first action of being ..."

– Albert Einstein 1944.

ONE

It was Sunday, April 4, 2026, 9:32 a.m. – coffee-jolt'n spicy pot cruller time for Carlo's mother, Bella. She and her CareBear©, named Bear, had just returned from a loping run along the crumbling runway where the old airport used to be. Bear was sitting in direct sunlight re-charging. Even the little departure lounge with its moldy velvet rope lines was under water now. Someone had made the executive decision to leave the last of the old prop planes standing on end of the runway – as if about to rev up its engines and take off. Someone's sick idea of funny. Now days you never know. Bella did have to laugh every time she and Bear ran past the big silver tail sticking up above the bayou water. She'd never been into sports or exercise, but after the death of her husband, Lenny, her A. I. CareBear©, had insisted she take up running. It hadn't taken much convincing. Bear had growled his opinion in his deep semi-modulated country western voice which was supposed to be irresistible to women. Really? But then, she thought, he actually had convinced her. In the catalogue, Bear's gravely voice is listed as 'low pick-up truck." You could choose from several voices for your bear, voices like Robert Redford or Ian McKellen. Some claimed the Frank Sinatra model A.I. CareBear© could sing Summer Wind and you couldn't tell the difference. Carlo would have chosen that Sinatra model for his mother, but it was out of stock as was every voice model except *pick-up truck*. There was a six-month back-order for Mr. Sinatra's horn. Carlo chose the pick up truck CareBear© because it could play air-guitar and sing "The Woods Are Full of Bears" like Jonny Cash.

Within a week of his arrival Bear had convinced Bella to take up running. Bear growled, "Ma'am, you don't need no ton a equipment fer runnin' … only a pair o short shorts, a t-shirt and runnin' sneaks. Gofer it, bitch!"

It had taken time, but Bella was sort of accustomed to what the 20 year-old set referred to as "filthy speak". In Bella's day, the word 'bitch' had been a curse word, funky at best. But over the years, a ton of bad words like 'suck', 'cocksucker' and 'fuck' had become part of everyday speech. There had even been a discussion on Jimmy Fallon of how it started when the word suck had gone from bad to good after rapper, Ratfukk Diddy, complained in his hit songs, "Suck So Good" and the even more popular, "It's A Suck-Bucket World", that getting sucked was actually a good thing, something everybody wanted, and wasn't it crazy-illin that folks should B using the suck word in such negative context? (FYI Ratfukk Diddy lost his copyright suit to musicians, Charles Strouse and Martin Charnin for copyright infringement on the tune "It's A Hard Luck Life" from the musical *Annie*.)

Bella's A.I. CareBear© was programmed with all the latest lingo as well as an ability to improvise, like when he said, "Bitches with assburgers shouldn't kiss witches wearing glass slippers!" Who comes up with these things? Actually, Bella once knew a woman named June who worked in the humor programing department at CareBear© headquarters whose job it was to think up unique and interesting speech patterns. She was hard to hold a normal conversation with. June sure got paid the big bucks thoough. But what she made was peanuts compared to the Injustani girls who came up with the "Life Sound" concept allowing your CareBear© to broadcast a Wi-Fi soundtrack to your life. Multi gazillionaire, those bitches! Went by the names, Bosom and Pretty and Tongue-Girl. Their idea was a sound system implanted in your CareBear's© chest which constantly surrounds its user with personally selected music, 24-7, playing just the right tunes that fit your activity and mood. "A sound track for your life," said Bosom, their spokeswoman, on their first holovision and smiling like the Cheshire Brat and showing more bosom than Bella thought appropriate for a young exec. More, at least, than Bella would be comfortable showing. But it's a young person's world.

You and anyone within five feet of your broadcast area heard your life music. "Life Sound" went crazy-ass viral. Bear helped Bella create her own soundtrack. Mostly sixties rock tunes like the Stones, Beatles, Sonny and Cher, Joni Mitchell, Leonard Cohen, Elton John, David Bowie, and a lot of classical – Ives, Bach, Brahms. And, of course, Johnny Cash.

After her coffee-jolt, and surrounded by a soft-blowing viola-squall of Beethoven, Bella looked forward to her daily shoulder/ neck massage from Bear. (To Sexual Healing with Marvin Gay)

When her son, Carlo, first bought the CareBear© for Bella, she'd told Carlo to take the stupid thing back. She didn't want it. She didn't need it. Said she had no room for electronic artificial intelligence in her life. But Carlo had insisted saying he couldn't take it back because it had already self-programed to Bella's DNA. Practically hard-wired itself. Pleading with his mother to keep it, Carlo put one of CareBear©'s exquisitely soft life-like paws in her hand.

"See! They're like little bunnies, Mom."

But Bella argued that Bear's big soft hairy vibrating teflo-rubber hands were nothing like human hands. Certainly nothing like her husband, Lenny's sweet sensuous touch.

"Dad's dead, Mom! Get jiggy with it." Carlo had said while Bear looked on with big brown eyes. Carlo gave her a hug. Then Bear hugged them both. That sealed the deal.

Yes, Lenny was dead. Seven years now. And over time, the soft sensuous touch of Bear's hands did grow on Bella as did all of Bear's features and functions including his foot-long tongue. First time Bear's tongue had a go at Bella it actually scared her. What the Hell is this slippery thing made of?

Bear had asked, "Do Miss Bella want Honey Dew Mellow lick-a-sikkel?" Thinking Bear was talking about a popsicle, Bella said, "Sure, whatever." Bear then proceeded to lick inside her ears and the nape of her neck working his way down to her belly and thighs and then...

Bella was old school. She didn't kiss and tell. Maybe it was simply that talking about very personal things embarrassed a woman of her age. Maybe it was that, unlike today's youth, she had boundaries. Anyway, she planned to someday e-write all this in a collection of short stories, or a novel maybe. A memoir. She would title it BOUNDARIES. Maybe young people today didn't have much in the way of boundaries, but Bella did. And she was proud of them.

Bear was giving Bella her post-run massage, his huge fingers vibrating their adjustable tingle and oscillating independently. Ten soft hairy vibrators, kneading and squeezing.

"Oh God." She moaned, "Oh God God God,"

Bella's eyes rolled back in her head. The CareBear© thing just got better and better. They said it would. These hairy machines were programmed to accommodate to their owner's personality and needs. The hairy aspect, the big sad hazel brown eyes – all tailored, like the ad said, to make each bear, "THE NEXT BEST THING TO A REAL BEST FRIEND. It learned and spoke with its owner's humor. It tickled Bella's funny bone... not, of course, as well as Lenny could make Bella laugh, but...

She was glad she'd named it simply...Bear. How original.

Bear was great because he understood humor – knew how to make her laugh by saying the unexpected. That's all good humor is, right? Her lady friends had asked if Bear was a he or a she? She checked. No anatomical sex package... of either gender. It was like a Ken Doll down there. Though it had no sex that she could see, it did make things tingle when it sang like Jonny Cash. So she called it a "he."

As her massage came to a close Bear asked with a Cambodian accent, "Bella want happy ending?"

She laughed out loud.

"No, Bella NOT want happy ending you stupid ...bear. And where did you learn that 'happy ending business'?" Bella asked giggling like a little girl.

"Online," Bear replied, "unbearablejokes.com"

"Well you certainly....."

But in the middle of her sentence a loud metallic shriek outside the window interrupted her – a noise like the pre-folding garbage trucks used to make early in the morning when they lifted those ten ton steel bins up and gobbled up their contents. Nowadays they're quiet. The nuke crew still makes noise, though, cooking what little garbage there is right on the spot before bag-feeding it to the good bacteria in the cess-truck. Surprising little smell. Something like cedar and ginger.

But this noise was different. A metal shriek. Ordinarily Bella liked to ride the loping bear, but she panicked and ran out to see what the racket was with Bear following behind. Bella forgot she'd told her son Carlo who'd moved in with her along with three of his friends after Lenny's passing that they could tear up the lawn in order to plant tomatoes.

She'd asked, "Who plants tomatoes anymore?"

Carlo said these were mutant hairlooms engineered to grow mature fruit the size of a grapefruit in just four weeks.

"I think you mean, heirlooms," Bear had corrected in a totally non-irritating voice. Bear was careful not to seem like a know-it-all (even though he did know it all)

Bella liked fresh tomatoes. She didn't care much for those new ones all the Foodie Stores sold today – big as watermelons. Tasted like watermelon rind. But they were sure enough fire engine red.

There, standing beside the rented soil-chew stood Carlo and his friends (housemates now) Slipper, Brain, and the girl everyone called The Hairy Colonizer. They wore work gowns, Ordinarily the young generation wore the equivalent of prom gowns. A lot of the guys wore the corsage and maxi man-tiara. This style became all the rage after teen transgender star, Florida-Girl, hit the e-waves with her mega-hit, *"I eat you like an Orange an spit out your pits'.* Florida-Girl wore a prom gown 24-7. Soon everyone was wearing prom gowns. High school seniors, of course, wore gowns on prom night. But now both boys and girls wore gowns...and they just kept wearing them. It was just one of those things.

Carlo held his holeo-homey-vid recorder focused on the damaged and smoking soil-chew lying on its side. Beside the smoking machine a dark cone protruded from the recently tilled Earth.

Carlo vidi-cammed everything hoping to catch useful and extraordinary footage for an extra credit project assigned him by his college Physics Professor, Mrs. Powers. His assignment was to show how physics should not be thought of as just the science of space, aliens, and Einstein's laws governing energy, time and matter, but also to show physical science was about everyday life.

Carlo looked up from his holeo-vid which whirred after clicking automatically to smart function. His light-metal life music lowered as he pointed his chain mail gloved finger at the glowing dull red cone and asked, "Hey Mom ...What the fukk is THAT?"

Bella had worked so hard to erase her memories. Suddenly they all flashed in her mind shooting up like bottle rockets, exploding, then slamming down to shatter on Bella's consciousness like those Notre Dame cathedral gargoyles hurled down on pedestrians by ISIL raiders last year. She and Bear had worked hours on end repressing her memories. Now they were all coming back. She stumbled and nearly fell.

These repressed memories were mainly of Lenny's and their life together – memories that for months after his death made her cry herself to sleep. Bear had been programmed by some of the best hacker psychos to help bury memories using acupuncture needles and Hymalayan up-beat pop.

But the sight of this "thing" on the lawn the kids had just unearthed forced Bella's memories to bubble up like alkaline geysers. She was nauseated by the rotten egg smell of her thawing memory. It always came from behind her eyes. Bear saw what was happening and hugged her tight against his furry chest but it was not enough to stop Bella from remembering that crazy night back 20 years ago when Lenny had been very much alive ...the night when they'd buried this ...thing.

Memories of her wonderful husband came flooding in. His vision seemed real as it kissed her cortex with warm soft hippocampus lips. Lenny's funny way with words came back too. That's when Bear did what he had to do – did what he'd been programmed to do. He bit Bella on the back of her neck. Hard. His red incisors showed he drew blood.

Bella spun on Bear. She was horrified.

"Jesus Christ! What the fu.....kk? " she snapped. Her music hit a high note that actually hurt Carlo's ears.

"Sorry, Ma'am. I had to do it," Bear said in his lowest sorriest country western twangy voice. Bella's life music started playing again – a duet with Pat Boone and Dolly Parton.

"Jeeziz! Don't you do ever that again!" she said.

Then she looked at the dark nose cone and whispered to her son, "Oh God, Carlo! Oh God."

TWO

Trying to get over Lenny's passing, Bella had worked with Bear. But she'd also followed a TV halobox spiritual healer named Jimmy Disciple – followed Jimmy Disciple's instructions for turning memories into dust and mist. Jimmy Disciple (or Jimmy D) hosted a daily 5pm self-help religious radio half-hour. She thought that by following Jimmy Disciple's simple breathing instructions she'd shattered her old memory discs. But now they were coming back together, reassembling like zombie puzzle pieces. They came back accompanied by the soundtrack of the life she'd lived back then – electric guitars and cowbells and giant drum solos. And then ... just this week when she'd prepared herself to finally meet Lenny's ghostly image for the first time in seven years ... someone else appeared. She was expecting her mind to call out from behind some curtain, her husband Lenny. She knew he wouldn't be real, but a re-creation from a million memories. She knew he wouldn't speak. Still, she was ready to confront her past ... and them move on.

But now, instead of Lenny, here was the image of the bearded man from twenty years ago. Here was the man with crazy frizzy hair, the one who'd been riding that thing whose nose cone was now poking out off the ground. The one with sickly pale skin and frizzy grey hair. His beard and hair had been wiry and unkempt. He wore clothes made from some strange shiny grey material.

In her mind's eye she beheld that crazy man who'd had been riding that damned thing when it crashed into her van twenty years ago. This was something her husband had told her to forget. All this forgetting. People were always telling her to forget the past. You can't change it, they said. Move on. Everybody was into forgetting nowadays. There were walk-in shops downtowns touting five-minute erasure. Almost every night Jimmy disciple and that little dog of his, Pedro, sang that little ditty...

"Forgetting what you know is the best form of letting go.
"Oh, you can't remember
What you just don't know
And most of your learning
Is just for show.
Forget all about it
Get ready to go
into the future
Where new memories grow.
Oh ... let your new memories grow."

But this thing poking out of the ground. That's what was bringing all her memories back. Bad and good. And it was true that many of her memories were wonderful. Like when she and Lenny first met in New York City. They'd both gone to the Big Apple searching for adventure and experience. They met at Gray's Papaya Juice Emporium on Forty Fourth Street where Lenny worked. Bella ordered a shake from Lenny. They'd fallen in Love. Just like that. Love at first sight. Soon they both had enough of New York's hustle and bustle, and were ready to move South. Southern to his soul, Lenny missed Bayou Culture. Bella was from Maine and was sick and tired of cold and snow so she loved the idea of retreating South with Lenny to Bayou Chien. Lenny drooled whenever he described bayou food to Bella, food like Y'at Nee Caja-burgers filled with oysters, crawfish, and hot pepper ground up with spiced pork and topped with a strip of alligator back loin arranged like a Japanese flower presentation (atop a beignet bun). He introduced her to possum strudel and water moccasin gumbo thick with prount beetle fillets.

Bella had been and still is a successful clay artist. What made her successful was her WILD WOMAN JURASSIC SHARDS which the art critic Borman Jewell-Doll once described as *"Jagged pieces of human society. The stuff aliens might find thousands of years after earth has burned to the ground."* She'd sold her WILD WOMAN JURASSIC SHARDS all over the South. Oh yes there'd been quarts of happy female serotonin flowing in her veins back then. She'd had no formal training. Maybe that was why people embraced her unique "shards." Her detractors called her an idiot-savant because, other than taking one adult evening pottery class, she was entirely self-taught. But she embraced criticism and claimed she was primitive by nature. She'd heard horror stories of Professors invading the creativity of students by giving top grades to students in their flocks who produced work just like theirs. They got the sheep 'A' grade. Wasn't that why they called them "schools" of art? The Hudson River School? The Dada school? No "schools" for Bella! There would be no mistake when folks looked at her clay art that it was made by anyone but her.

She wanted it to be the only clay art in the world that looked like the wild woman from Bayou Cheine smash-mold-squeezed and kneaded fresh-dug clay into celebrations of female dance-happiness.

She and Lenny had an arrangement. Lenny would take care of baby Carlo and the dog and the goat and he would make dinner along with doing a thousand household chores while Bella made pottery. Hell, Bella was the breadwinner selling in galleries all across America as well as at snooty craft shows like at The Rhinebeck N.Y. Craft Fair outside The Big Apple. She would come home from shows with her pockets full of fifty-dollar bills. She sold down South during the winter months in Coconut Grove, Ft. Lauderdale, Las Olas, and Orlando. In the beginning the whole family would accompany Bella on show junkets up and down the East Coast. She got invited to display in all the big Craft Fairs of that era ...everywhere except The New Orleans Jazz and Culture festival which was less than a hundred miles away.

Each year Bella submitted slides of her Wild woman Shards to this New Orleans Heritage and Jazz Festival hoping the judges would consider her worthy of showing with them. But each year the New Orleans art-judges rejected her. Finally Bella tried something new. She re-named her shards "F sharp Jazzy Shards" and wonder upon wonder, she was accepted. Mid April 1977 she loaded up the van, kissed Lenny and their dog, Laphonso, and the goat, James Joyce, and sweet Carlo good-bye then drove off to the Big Easy loaded with Blue Bayou Fossil F sharp Jazzy Shard Pottery.

Lenny was alive at that time. He asked for just one thing – could she please buy a New Orleans famous Y'at Nee Caja-burger, take it back to her hotel room and phone him while she ate it. He had not eaten one since their wedding. He wanted her to describe each munch, lick, and swallow. Could she please do that for him? Could she please give him a full-mouthed description of his favorite N'O'leans taste treasure? At first Bella thought he was being funny. But, no, Lenny really wanted to hear his wife's saliva slurps – wanted to imagine her mouth heat closed tight and juicy around that stunning sandwich. Lenny wanted to hear moans and groans bordering on phone sex.

"Really? You want to hear me eat? That's what you want?" asked Bella.

"You got a problem with that? I'm going to be left alone here for a week. It's the least you can do," he whined.

Bella left on a Monday afternoon. When she got to New Orleans she called and confessed she had not been able to find the famous sandwich. In fact, she said whenever she described that Y'at Nee Caja-burger to anyone who would listen, no one had a clue what she was talking about. Jokingly Lenny said it was probably on account of southerners not being able to understand Bella's thick Maine accent. This was certainly possible, as Bella herself could not understand the Southerner's thick patois. Grampa Joe for example. Forget it! But still, she'd promised Lenny that come "Helen in Highwater," she WOULD find and eat this crazy spice-aromatic hot atomic neon caja-burger for him and describe it bite by bite. And he'd better have put Carlo to bed by the time she phoned because she planned on giving her husband a litany of kissing tongue-dance sensuous seductive luscious adjectives. But the following night and every night thereafter when she phoned,

Bella told Lenny once again she had not been able to find that stupid burger.

Bella had made a lot of artsy friends over the years on the show circuit. New Orleans is a party town. These exhibitors had a slew of nighttime soirees lined up after the fair ended each day where plates of crawfish, gumbo and pulled pork got scarfed. Sometimes she was too full to out looking for Lenny's sandwich.

"Atomic Freddy's," Lenny shouted into the phone one night. "Go to Atomic Freddy's! That's where they make the best ... on Browning Street. You go down there and I promise you'll see what I'm talking about!"

So on the last day of the Jazz fest, when business was slow while the crowd was being dazzled by Chick Corea, Bella headed downtown Big Easy in her rainbow van asking along the way for directions to Atomic Freddy's on Browning Street. She was determined.

She got a little disoriented along the way so she stopped at a cafe on Beale Street. A waiter was out sweeping the deck. She parked the van on the street in front so she could keep an eye on it. This was, after all, New Orleans – Crimetown U.S.A. She'd gone up to the bearded waiter who sported a shaved skull with a smiling skull tattooed on top of his head and asked, "I was hoping to get a ... and I hope I'm pronouncing this right ... a N'at Nee Cajacheeseburger?"

The waiter scratched his tattooed head. The skull's smile and the waiter's smile were similar ... like brothers from another mother. Was there irony in a tattoo having more teeth than it's owner? And what was the relevance of crossed Japanese swords, anchors, and dragons tattooed on each of his arms below the dagger-pierced red heart of MOM needled across his left bicep?

The waiter had uttered through alarming tooth vacancies, "Baby, maybe y'all be talking bout a Universal Muffaletto?"

Both skulls, the waiter's and his tattoo's, were grinning as he continued, "Listen to me, Sugar ... here's what you wanna gonna do in order t' git y'rself over to Browning Street. Y'all jes' follow this here street to the end and then ... take ... a ... a ... right ... I think. Or is it a left? Let me think ..."

Bella sat down to jot his directions on a newspaper when a police cruiser crawled up stopping only a few feet behind her van. The mashed potato jowled cop who was driving growled unintelligibly at his radio static while his partner – a black lady cop with Scarlett O'Hara-red lipstick and varnished short straight black hair, struggled to hoist her fat ass out. With leather holster squeaking, radio and nightstick flapping, she shook herself like a dog to re-settle excess fat inside her tight fitting police shirt. Her navy blue cop-issue slacks were tight to bursting forcing a lump of muffin-top jiggle-flesh to pop out above her hips.

As she slammed the cruiser door her eyes shot sparks at the waiter's bloodshot slits. With surprising agility she hop-stepped up onto the deck to stab her finger at his chest hissing, "Now ... don't you go saying I din't warn you, Tommy Don! Don you try an give me none o' dat shit!"

And without warning she punched him between mouth and nose with a small hard fist making a flat squishy noise. He staggered back, one hand holding his nose. He studied the stream of blood squirting into his hand while holding

17

his other hand outstretched trying to protect against the flurry of lady punches which followed.

Maybe it was because Bella had never seen a real fist fight before that it horrified her so. Was it the violence of sloppy slipping wild-ass punches thrown – mostly by the lady cop at the collapsed waiter. Her punches struck his jaw and temple. Her fist glanced off tattooed forearms, shoulder and skull. Like ballet slippers, the lady cop's patent leather shoes scraped the floor wheeling and prancing a violent pain-infused devil's dance. The blows she delivered were so very different from the clean punches of a TV boxing match.

"Is you gonna go resisting arrest again, motherfucker?" she finally asked after a right cross to the jaw made his knees buckle.

Taking his silence for resisting arrest she punched his head three times in rapid succession. *Thuck thuck thuck.* The waiter's skull tattoo began to bleed. A cat's cradle of slime-red mucous strings hung from his mouth where his few teeth clung to diseased gums. The cop exhausted herself with a series of kicks to the tattoo dragon on his neck as he tried to protect himself by curling into a fetal ball.

High-pitched and nearly hysterical now, she screamed, "Stay down asshole! Listen to me. (*pant pant*) I don't ever … never … want to see your sorry ass in my neighborhood again … (*pant*) If I do I swear I'll …"

The Lady Cop had run out of breath and was unable to finish her sentence. She was bent over at the waist with both fists balled and resting on her knees.

Bella tried to hide behind her newspaper. She'd been afraid of cops all her life after taking part in an anti Vietnam War protest where she got whacked from behind by a cop's

Billy club. It had left her unconscious and bleeding in the street. What alarmed her most, though, was that some cowardly part of her mind had already made the decision that if it came down to choosing sides here she would join the lady cop. Absolutely. She'd have justified it out of self-protection because, well, she had a family to think about, didn't she? She had a child, right? A husband and a dog and a goat. But then she thought, what kind of person am I? The cowardly child in her brain whined how a man with tattoos like this waiter probably had it coming. But, did he? She only knew she did not want to get involved. She was not prepared to intervene and possibly get beaten like the waiter. She imagined poor Lenny getting a phone call telling him his wife was in jail ... or the hospital. He'd freak out!

The angry cop stood with legs apart above the waiter like she about to urinate on him. You never know. People do crazy things in the heat of battle. What crazy history did these two have? Bella only knew she wanted no part of getting caught in the middle of it.

The cruiser door opened. The older fat officer, a ringer for J. Edgar Hoover, slid his fat ass out.

"Ellen!" he called, "Either kill him or kiss him! Let's go!"

She had a name. Ellen. She was not just some Robocop. Ellen from Hell'n back didn't immediately acknowledge her partner. So he trundled his lard-ass over and gently lay a meat hook on her shoulder saying, "C'mon Ellen. He's not worth it. C'mon now. Let's go. "

The J. Edgar Hoover look-alike escorted Ellen back to the hot idling Blade Runner of a cruiser with its loaded shotguns and crackling radio. The two cops then sped away like they do in the movies with Bella and the bleeding waiter watching them disappear around the corner.

The temperature had been a balmy seventy-one ... a beautiful spring day. Bella could smell fresh blooming lilacs as she stumbled over to the waiter extending her hand to help him to his feet.

"Cops are crazy in this town," he'd said, "People don' know how bad they is!"

"Right," said Bella. She wanted to explain to him that she was in town just having some fun and making a little money and maybe listen to the jazz go down – Chick Corea, Herby Hancock. She had a family ... a kid and a husband waiting on her sandwich report, for Christ sake.

oThe waiter continued, "Y'all go crossin' cops in this town, man, they'll fuk you. They'll kill you soon as look at you!"

"I'm not ... I'm just ... you know, want to find that Atomic Burger." Bella quietly said.

After settling the waiter in a chair Bella walked to her van and sat inside it decompressing. Then she'd looked at her newspaper with the directions the crazy tattooed waiter had given before he'd run afoul of the wrong arm of the law.

THREE

Bella took off from in front of the café and immediately got lost. She was so rattled she couldn't locate her position on a New Orleans City map. She pulled over to ask a tall man for directions. The man obliged in a soprano voice. When Bella realized the man was a woman she lost focus and forgot what she–he'd said. Bella was from Maine. There were no transvestites in Maine!

She asked a few more people on the street but no one could help. Finally she found a U.P.S. driver. He'd know. But now Bella had her gender radar up and running. She was unable to take her eyes off the long lashes of the man in Brown ... was this a he or a she, this woman in Brown? He - she certainly was pretty enough. Bella wrote what she could recall of the UPS "dude's" instructions on her Newspaper below those of the waiter ... directions that involved circling around dead-end and one-way (the wrong way) streets. The UPS driver's sweet-voiced question kept repeating in Bella's head, "You sure ya'll ain't wantin' no muffaletto? Ya sure now? Cause I can show y'all a nice muff-lettooooooooooo real easy."

Bella drove aimlessly on streets that were more like alleys – too small for cars, let alone her van. She'd asked for directions again and heard, "Dis paat o' Browning you're looking for, do you know if dat's a street or is it a lane? See, it do makes a difference."

Bella smiled and shrugged. She came to a road construction crew leaning on shovels. Leaning out her window she'd asked a big black man in yellow hard hat holding the lollipop stop-go sign on a pole, "Have you, by any chance, ever heard of an Atomic Cajun Burger ... or a place called the Elusive Bayou ... no, I'm sorry, it's called Atomic Freddy's? And it's on Browning Street."

The bastard had responded with a lip sneer that meant, "What the Hell you talking bout, Lady?"

The lollipop sign man had stuck his face in her window and said, "You gots to keep moving, Ma'am. You can't be holding up no traffic!"

Bella was at wit's end. She started to cry as the large black man bellowed a steaming stream of unintelligible directions through lips squeezed tight with impatience, "Y'all jus keep going dat way ... dat way ... over dere where dat canal be at! Y'all see where I'm pointin'? Y'all jus keep going t'da odder side dere!"

Bella wiped her eyes and drove off.

"The other side of the canal." That's what he said. She'd have to be satisfied with that. But she'd driven two blocks before she realized she'd left her newspaper with her directions on it with the big man who at this time was listening to his buddy, "Why you tell dat lady Browning Street over dere? It back de udder way! I'm sure it is!"

Both men scratched their heads. At the same time Bella, several blocks away, scratched her head. This head scratching business, when did humans start scratching like this when they wondered something? It must have been early in evolution when humanoids had thinner skulls. Did rubbing and scratching the head literally stimulate the brain, the memory? That made sense. Bella wondered if it was just her who always lost her lists, her notes, her maps. And why did she always lose the one list she needed most while every other worthless scrap of paper, old lists, receipts, tissues, Fudgsicle wrappers, all settled onto the floor of her car never to disappear. Was there a group or a subspecies who never lost their lists and directions? OCD people? Would she ever become one of those successful women her mother always talked about?

Bella was moving through light traffic. She knew she was flying by the seat of her pants. The street had changed names three times. She had the sense she was driving in circles. She'd gotten funneled into curious arcs by so many one-way streets. But hadn't she just crossed over a canal? That had to be a good sign... unless it was the same canal she'd crossed over ten minutes ago.

And then she was deep inside a maze of tiny lanes inside the city. She'd lost all track of time. Had it been an hour? It couldn't be two hours, could it? As a statement against mental slavery to time, Bella never wore a watch. The street she was on kept getting narrower and narrower until there was barely a foot of clearance on each side of her van. Finally the alley ended at a confluence of trashcans. A derelict Desoto up on blocks negated any further progress. Leaning against the Desoto was a torn mattress soiled with what looked like old dried blood.

When she realized she'd have to reverse the van out of the blind alley she felt like crying. But she bucked up and hung her head out the window. Tight against a building she was clueless on her passenger side. Slowly, literally crawling backwards, she was hoping not to hit anything or anyone. She'd almost made it. She was sighing with relief when the van seemed to explode with a terrible metal ripping sound.

That's when Bella remembered en her whole world coming apart.

FOUR

Out on the lawn, Slipper, The Hairy Colonizer, Brain, Bear, and Carlo could almost see each thawing memory swirling about Bella's face like Saturn's moons.

Slipper whispered to Carlo, "Is your mother okay? She's scaring me."

Bella remembered it all now – the van shaking with an explosive crash. Almost immediately a second terrifying metallic thud slamming her head against the window post. Her window had cracked. She'd lost consciousness for an instant. She remembered the ligaments in her neck burning when she woke. Her heart was beating fast. In the rear view mirror she could see a wild looking frizzy-haired man, a senior citizen, as she'd later call him. Their eyes met in the mirror. Bella clearly remembered his dark blue t-shirt covered with yellow stars. Or had they been Saturns? After retrieving his spectacles off the street he struggled to upright some kind of bicycle – this same thing which the kids had partially dug up. She remembered it having wings – no. What were they? They were more like rotors. Was it an ultra light? The handlebars had been bent in the crash – nearly doubled back. He'd straightened them. He was trying to start it. But it only made a strange high whine. She would certainly never forget the big thatch of eyebrows over the man's wild bulging eyes. The thin gnome-like man had cursed, then shoved the bike contraption to the ground abandoning it before hobbling down the alley in the direction from which he'd come.

A minute earlier Bella had been hoping someone might come along to help her reverse the van out the alley. Not a soul was there. Now people were everywhere – leaking out from doorways and alleys like zombie monkeys. All seemed to have that slack-jawed inbred Southern look.

Then she noticed all eyes focused under the passenger side of her van – back by her right rear tire. She twisted in her seat to see what they were looking at. Her back hurt. Her neck hurt. Whiplash?

Jesus! All she'd wanted to do was to eat some stupid sandwich. Was that too much to ask? It wasn't even for her. It was for Lenny. Poor dear Lenny.

She surfaced from her memories. How she missed him now standing out on the lawn overcome by memories brought on by that thing. She felt an electric belly tingle of fear. She hated being afraid like some little girl.

A few of the gawkers back then had been holding their hands covering their mouths in shock. Not a good sign. In shock over what? She knew she hadn't hit anyone or anything. On the contrary, something had hit her. Christ, she hadn't even been moving.

Cautiously, she'd opened the door wide enough to slide from her seat to the sidewalk. People stared. She'd walked around toward the back of the van to see what everyone was staring at. At first she couldn't see anything. Then ... Oh Dear Sweet Mother of Jesus! From under the van two black leather boots had been sticking out – twitching.

FIVE

Her memory had such detail. A police motorcycle lay on its side still running. Its rear wheel was spinning like crazy. Bella's van had two huge dents in the side and a long ugly black tire smear.

Newly arriving spectators gasped. A woman whispered, "Holy mother of God!"

A man claiming to be a marine medic had commandeered a few good men to pull the body out. He was yelling, "You fellas! Help me out here. Grab him by his boots! Okay now, one ... two ... three!"

It had taken some questionable yanking. And though not a medically sanctioned method, they'd succeeded in pulling out the cop. His head and hands had been limp and flopping. A surly teen shut off the cop's motorcycle engine. The Marine doctor put his ear to the cop's mouth to check for breath then looked up beyond the crowd beseeching the white puffy clouds in a soft war-weary voice, "Thank you, sweet Lord Jesus ... he's alive!"

The tattooed waiter's words had begun echoing in her head... "Y'all go crossin' cops in this town ... man, they gonna fuk you up!"

The memory of this unconscious cop's face was burned into her mind. Then ... the cop's lips twitched. His eyes fluttered. They opened. He was spitting blood. His helmet lay beside him. He'd tried to sit up, his big shaky hands gripping the curb and the medic's shoulder. He'd puked on his own leg. He'd looked around bewildered like an earthquake victim Bella had seen on TV.

The Marine "doctor" or medic or whatever he was started waving his hand in front of the cop's face asking how many fingers.

"What's your name?" the medic kept asking.

With some effort he'd said, "Harold...Harold Adams."

But the cop's eyes slowly closed and again he toppled onto his side sending his gun clattering across the street. It had been a strange weapon. Bella's father had been a gun collector. She knew guns. She'd never seen a weapon like that with its bulbous hand grenade handle covered with dials and wire coils. A homeless man with bad teeth and a protruding lisping tongue had timidly pushed the strange pistol with his foot toward the cop. He'd seemed afraid to touch the gun. With the help of the medic, Harold was sitting in an upright position. She remembered the cop had picked up the gun and tried to jam the gun back in his holster, but fumbled. After that he kept it in his hand.

The cop had finally asked in a hoarse whisper, "Someone want to tell me what the Hell just happened."

SIX

It was all coming back now, the motorcycle cop's strange uniform – not your typical New Orleans Officer's blue shirt with epaulets and badge like the two cops at the café wore. This cop's uniform was made from some sleek fabric – silky like a parachute – teal blue with golden-yellow lightning bolts sewn in metallic gold threads on the epaulettes. Amazingly, it had not gotten ripped or damaged even after sliding under her van. His badge had been covered with tiny writing – not like anything Bella had ever seen. And even though UPC bar codes were just then coming out, this cop's badge had a bar code instead of a badge number. And his nametag said, Harold. Why only his first name?

No one had cellspeak back then. They didn't even have cell phones – just big bulky phones in a briefcase. The cop's radio was broken so a thick man with pig eyes and a Foo Mon Choo mustache had run inside a bodega to call an ambulance. And that was another thing – his radio. It was different than anything Bella had ever seen – a mess of splintered black plastic now littering the sidewalk, but it had all these wires and diodes too. The earpiece had been hanging like a spider emitting odd undulating tones like a HAM radio.

The pig face man announced to the cop, "Your buddies are on their way – the ambulance crew!"

29

Bella remembered the Foo Man Choo man – the way his porcine arms and chest had been squeezed inside a t-shirt two sizes too small – white with a black cannon on wheels firing a stylized red fireball with the words "Gettysburg 50,000 dead."

The cop had had looked up with anger and asked Pig Man, "Who told you to call anyone?"

Pig man shrugged. "Sorry, I ... I ... just ... !"

The cop named Harold looked over where his black Harley lay oozing oil and gas.

As if reading the cop's thoughts, The Marine Medic and Pig Man walked to the motorcycle. It must have weighed five hundred pounds. But they'd stood it up on its kickstand.

Seeing his motorcycle upright, the cop, helmetless, his stringy hair sweaty and plastered to his scalp, staggered to his feet. He'd mounted the bike like a drunk while the Doctor and Pig Man held it steady. They tried to reason with him. "For your own good, sir. You need to lie down. C'mon now! We need to make sure you're okay,"

Bella remembered the cop sneering and trying to brush them away with his leather-gloved fist. But this upset his balance and the Harley once again fell over. The cop took the weight of the fall on his shoulder. He lay on his side groaning. Blood trickled from his ear. He'd lain there a good half-minute before looking around like he was waking up from a bad dream. He'd murmured, "Hey ...Where's that old man, the bearded guy? You know, the guy I was chasing. You didn't let him get away, did you?"

The doctor and Pig Man had looked at each other. Had Bella been the only one to see the bearded man?

"Uh ... I guess if you're talking about the guy who was driving that motor scooter thing ... yeah ... I don't know. He must -a took off. But his machine – it's over there. It's toast! That's it over there!" said Pig Man pointing to twisted steel tubes, skids and wires and two very thin yet surprisingly undamaged rotors. Bella had realized then it was not a bicycle or a scooter.

That's when the cop asked the question Bella had been dreading, "Who owns the van?"

Everyone had stared at Bella. Earlier there had been the occasional finger pointed at her when someone arrived and asked what was going on. Some seemed surprised she was still there. Was it obvious to everyone but Bella she should have abandoned her van, high-tailed it to the greyhound station and caught the first bus out of town?

She'd wondered if being a woman would help? She recalled how shaky and frail her voice had sounded in her own ears ... subservient like in the fifth grade when, under duress, she'd admitted to the principal she'd been the one who'd called the cafeteria cashier lady a bitch. Back then she'd instinctively known to cry in front of power like some sorry puppy peeing on itself. Because she'd gone all submissive, the principle hadn't called her mother.

"It's my van, sir!" she'd whined.

The cop then looked at her like she was some odd fish he'd just brought up in his net – something he might fillet. Would he cook her with head on? Bella's mind had gone silly on her – perhaps to release the strain.

Bella remembered the insignia above the bar code on the cop named Harold's shirt – like a Saturn with rings. The cop had seen her staring.

31

"What the Hell you looking at?" he'd barked, "What are you doing here anyway?"

She was scared and started trying to explain. But her stammering about the sandwich and the Jazz sounded crazy even to her. The cop was now looking at the side of her van – at the black tire marks surrounding bare and crushed metal.

The cop was saying, "Hey lady! I asked you a simple ..." But he hadn't finished his question because they all heard sirens in the distance.

The cop pointed to the fallen scooter or fly-mo-bicycle or whatever it was and said, "Listen ... just do what I tell you. You men – throw that thing in the garbage."

Three men tried but it was too large for the dumpster. He changed his order and said, "Throw it in the back of the lady's van! Okay, with you, lady? "

Bella had nodded vigorously. She'd hurried to throw open the van's back doors. It took a while but with shoving and scraping, the men in the crowd managed to get the contraption inside with only its rear end hanging out. She heard pieces of her pottery break but said nothing. Collateral damage. As soon as Bella roped the doors tight against the mangled contraption, the cop fired up his Harley. Before he took off he'd said over his shoulder, "None of this ever happened! You hear me? I mean it!"

Bella watched the cop wobble away down the alley on a bent front rim nearly clipping the curb. Pig Man whispered to her, "I'd get out of here if I was you!"

Men then guided Bella as she backed the van around. She'd driven off just as cop cars began arriving with their red and blue lights flashing and sirens wailing. It had begun to rain. Her last look in her rearview mirror showed not a soul on the street. Two minutes earlier there'd been forty or fifty. She went back to the fair to dismantle her pottery stand. Most of it she chucked. Without having tasted one single Universal Atomic Neon Cajun Burger she'd sped up the ramp, got on rt. 90 West and headed out of town.

An hour and thirty-five minutes later Bella had pulled into her driveway. Rain was coming down hard. Amid flashes of lightning she'd run sobbing into Lenny's arms.

SEVEN

Bella told Carlo. "Keep digging. There's more still buried."

"How do you know?" asked Carlo.

"Because your father and I buried it!" she said.

"What the fuck, Mom ... what' are you talking about?" asked Carlo.

"That thing. It's some kind of flying ... bicycle or scooter," said Bella.

"Well, that makes just about no sense," said Carlo using a certain tone of voice a son reserves for his mother. He and his friends stared at the throbbing red carbonized tip protruding from the broken sod. Carlo took his holeovid off smart-shoot and resumed manual focus to record the scene. Then he photographed his friends, Brain, Slipper and The Hairy Colonizer standing around the damaged tiller. They wore soiled work dresses. He photographed his mother. Stacked neatly behind her were eight bags of whole-ground bacterial organic soil and a dozen Potted Jupiter tomato plants waiting to go in the ground. Carlo couldn't remember when you still could grow real tomatoes – before the blight came. He could sort of remember the sweet acid tomato taste. The sales lady said it only took 30 days before these Super Juper, Baby Janes would be ready to eat!

They all lived in Bella's house. Despite Bella's friends' disapproval, she'd allowed, even welcomed Carlo to live at home ... and she'd invited Carlo's friends to share her home. Bella's friends had told her in no uncertain terms that letting these kids move in would be one whopper of a motherly indulgence she would regret. Her friends had rolled their over-painted eyes and said Carlo's friends weren't kids anymore. They were young adults. And did she see what they were wearing? Prom dresses! Seriously. And two of them were young women: Slipper and The Hairy Colonizer. Bella's friends quoted Madame Frangois, the snide new right wing President of France who said, "Trouble is a bitch and a bitch is trouble." Or something like that. They still spoke French over there and probably always will. But Bella didn't care about French opinions.

And it wasn't like Carlo had planned offering his friends living space in his mother's house. It just happened...organically. First he'd invited Brain to stay for a week or two – at least until Brain found a place of his own. Brain's real name was Brian, but Brian got misspelled 'Brain' on his freshman nametag. It stuck because he was a nerd. A week became a month. Turned out Bella liked Brain's sense of humor. And he was handy with repairs. He could do electricity, plumbing, even carpentry! These were things bear was not good at. And Brain was so cute in his green prom gown. And there was this too – Bella had overheard Brain on the phone offhandedly describing her to one of his friends, "She's got golden blond hair that's turning a little grey because she worries so much. But she's very pretty. And she's got these strong hands ... like a farmer's wife. She's got a bucktooth rosy smile and wears no lipstick. I'll tell you what, Dude! I'd sure as Hell like to find a girl my age who looks like Bella and is funny like her."

On top of all that Bella liked Brain's music, his computo-techno rock. So, of course Bella allowed Brain to stay. What woman alive can resist compliments? Ask any CareBear©. AIs shamelessly spout compliments to men and women alike like spritzer fountain cones.

Next to move in was the girl everybody called The Hairy Colonizer. Her real name was Janis. Like many young women after the great anti-cosmetic movement of 2018 The Hairy Colonizer believed a woman should never, not ever shave her body hair. She kept herself relatively clean, but Bella's friends kept warning Bella that This Janis girl – this Hairy Colonizer as everyone called her – had what folks called 'a wild hair' growing out her butt. And had she heard This Hairy Colonizer's accompanying bacteriological life music score? Yoiks! Like a million tiny bugs singing rap! So Bella did what she had to do. She stopped seeing her friends.

Bella told The Hairy Colonizer she could stay for a week, but The Hairy Colonizer turned out to be such an excellent cook who knew everything there is to know about yogurt, and she was such a very sweet girl, and Bella had no daughter of her own. And, as Bella really had been dreading rattling around the big house all by her self, she gave the okay for The Hairy Colonizer to move into one of the upstairs bedrooms.

Last of Carlo's friends to move in was Slipper. Bella couldn't make up her mind which of these girls, Slipper or The Hairy Colonizer, would be more the daughter she'd have had if she'd had one. This daughter that Bella never had would probably have had dirty bitten fingernails like Slipper. Slipper was thin but surprisingly strong. She was not super brainiac-smart like The Hairy Colonizer. Slipper's music aura was straight out of the 90s. Courtney Love, Madonna, Cindi Lauper, Alanis Morrissett, Melissa Ethridge. And like both girls, Bella's daughter would have been unlucky in love. Slipper wore her heart on her sleeve – literally – fourteen broken heart tattoos, seven on each forearm, one for each boyfriend who'd gone smelly rotten, gone missing, or had simply dumped her.

She got the name Slipper after her last boyfriend, a creep named Herr Art Wolf, the vunder-kinde artist from Germany, broke off their relationship when Slipper refused, of all things, to change out of the fuzzy monkey slippers she wore to his art opening.

"Ya! You VILL be putting on some decent footwear to go vits za gown you are vearing for my opening, my dear! And shut up now. I don't vant to be hearink another word out of your mouse."

It wasn't that simple, of course. Nothing ever was with Herr Art Wolf. Everyone agreed he was metaphorically riding that upward spiral-bound art-fame elevator. He'd bet everything on becoming the bejeweled set's latest darling. He painted, rather, he I-phone-painted text-interpretations of Ed Munch's Scream painting. Ah, The Scream, what a concept. Herr Art Wolf designed his own phone hack-app program which copied, pasted, and projected Munch's screamer with open mouth actually screaming and spinal-dancing in 3-d everywhere you can imagine including atop The Notre Dame Cathedral only days before The ISIL Gargoyle attack. Some wisenheimer nitt-bag wrote in the art-junk maga-journal, *Artifarct*, that Herr Art Wolf's interpretation of Munch's screamer looked more like King Kong. But wasn't there always someone trying to be first saying the new emperor has no clothes? That said, Herr Wolfe was no fluff-bag. He immediately collage-paste-projected the screamer atop the bell tower of Notre Dame yelling out Big Brother and the Holding Company's sixties hit, Take Another Little Piece Of My Heart, which he'd downloaded off Slipper's collection. Slipper got it from Bella. Herr Art Wolf depicted the famous actress, Gaby Hoffman in a circle like a clock face surrounding Munch's iconic Screamer singing Joplin's words as well! And within a month Herr Art Wolf had the screamer bellowing out from Martha Raye's giant gaping mouth as she dove to her death from the pre-doomed photo-shopped Twin Towers Herr Art Wolf depicted sinking below the Dubai skyline.

"Top that, bitches!" Herr Art Wolf was caught saying on a hot mike by a drone spyder-phone.

They say Herr Art Wolfe was himself responsible for starting the rumor that he was brought up by wild dogs in West Berlin. To many this accounts for his obsession with always being meticulously dressed. The night of his big opening he wore a silver and yellow plaid Brooks Brothers Hillary Clinton pants suit with black patent leather shoes. He'd paid through the nose for Pee Wee Herman's bow tie which he wore over the buttoned neck of his certified star-owned Cathy Griffith black shirt. He was most proud, however, of his fine Italian ostrich Crocs © which reportedly cost twenty thousand euros. He is quoted by the interviewer from *Judas Priest*, "Man! Zey feel like God's lips making love to my feets."

Statements like this won Slipper's and the art-world's heart. At least in the beginning. But fame, like a rotting houseguest, lasts only three days before it starts to smell.

Slipper and Herr Art Wolf's breakup was inevitable. The more fame Herr Art Wolf basked in, the fewer beautiful concept paintings came out of his Fahrvergnugen brain and phone. It was after being hospitalized for binge-eating sauerbraten on a bet with the Austrian Prince, Schnauvel Brautsweiner, that Herr Art Wolf's dyspepsia cause gastric juice to burp into his esophagus injuring his imagination. Herr Art Wolf's creativity, from that point on according to Slipper, seemed to dry it up like that desiccated salt lake in California where a steamboat still lays stranded in the sand in the middle on its side. The more notoriety he acquired the sourer he became and the more he demanded that Slipper's non-conformity conform to his rise in stature. His fame festered like a boil on the art-world's ass until it came to a head the night of Herr Art Wolf's big opening at the Rothsgard Gallery. To his credit, his scream images came to life on every foot of wall space. Earplugs against the screams were issued at the door as a precaution.

Trouble began when Glen Beck's granddaughter, Liz Cheney Beck, who'd become one of many newly obsessed fans of Herr Art Wolf, came to his big opening drunk. She'd gotten drunker as the evening wore on and when she tried to drape herself on Herr Art Wolf he pushed her away. Sloshed and bellicose Ms. Beck became loud and ugly just as the most important art critic in New Orleans, Pieater Jellodoll walked in. Jellodoll had been scheduled to review Herr Art Wolfe's show for the ultra snoot-bag rag, *Art Boaster Magazine*.

Ms. Liz Cheney Beck went straight toward Jellodoll as he was bragging to Herr Art Wolf, "You know, they say I can smell good art."

Herr Art Wolf tried to drag Ms. Liz Cheney Beck away. She stumbled and fell at Slipper's feet...on Slipper's fuzzy monkey slippers. (one could barely see them under the long sleeveless sky blue prom gown Slipper wore) Slurring wickedly Ms. Beck said rather too loud, "Sooooo, Honey ... are those your blow-job slippers ... the ones Herr Art Wolf told you to wear when you his balls?" I mean, you are the Wolf's bitch, aren't you? You do what he tells you, right?"

Slipper tried to ignore Ms. Beck.

But Liz Cheney Beck was like a dog with a sock in his mouth. Wouldn't let it go. She said, "Honey ...you are Herr Art Wolfe's bitch, aren't you?"

"I'm sorry. I couldn't hear you," replied Slipper politely.

"Well, this show is all about screams and screaming bitches, right?" said Liz slurring her words. Liz's gown was tight and pushed her bosoms up and out until most of her monkey-paw tattooed nipples jiggled out the top.

She said, "Oh sooo soooorrrry!"

Liz got to her feet and said to Jellodoll, "Hey, Mr. Big Shot, what do you think of thish little Princesses dumb ass slippers? Would you like her to tickle your balls with them later? I'm sure if you asked nice ... "

Jellodoll tried to move away. But the Beck woman wasn't about to let him go. She stumbled after him and tackled him from behind. They hit the floor.

Herr Art Wolf saw Jellodoll go down. He dropped his paper cup and minced to where Jellodoll lay wrapped in the arms of Liz Cheney Beck. He pulled the art critic free and helped Jellodoll to his feet saying, "I am so ... so sorry, Herr Jellodoll. I am just so sorry."

But Jellodoll was having none of it. He whimpered something about slippers and left the gallery.

Herr Art Wolf looked stunned. Then he collected himself and approached Slipper. Though none of it was her fault he began screaming at Slipper, "Getttttt outtttt ... Geh rausss mit choo! Justttt getttttttt outttt uff my life!"

Next day his screaming photo would take up the whole front page of the Miami Herald's Art section with the headline, "Screamer interpretist screams loud!"

He even made the New York Times with the headline, "Wolf cries Wolf!"

Out on the street Slipper bought a gyro from a vender before wandering aimlessly for an hour. She ran into Carlo who happened to be out walking Laphonso. Slipper and Carlo had been friends since High school.

"S'up?" asked Carlo.

"Long story. You don't want to know," Slipper replied. But she quickly relented and relayed the evening's events ending by admitting she had no place to go.

"C'mon, I'll ask my mom if you can stay with us," Carlo suggested.

And, long story short, Bella invited Slipper to stay with them for as long as she liked.

Slipper wore slippers all the time after that, even when taking Laphonso for walks. Unlike Laphonso, Slipper avoided puddles. She also tried to stay on lawns and moss so as not to wear them out.

"Slippers have delicate souls ... like humans," she liked to say.

But she really didn't care if her slippers got holes or got wet or wore out. She'd just bicycle to The Salvation Army and get a new pair and maybe pick up a used prom dress. It didn't matter if she bought clown slippers or slippers like stuffed lions, cats or dogs ... my little pony, Hello Kitty, whatever. She bought them cheap. She didn't earn much money part time waitressing at The Mush Room Tavern and Bar. She didn't care if the right matched the left either. Her favorite became fuzzy bears because they made Bear laugh. And she loved hearing the big bear laugh.

EIGHT

"Can I ... like, do anything for you?" Brain asked Bella. Brain had a small grass clipping in his beard. Ordinarily Bella would have laughed and pulled it out. But Bella just stared, lost in thought.

Bear lumbered over and plucked the piece of grass from Brain's beard.

"Thanks Bear."

Attempting to pull the contraption with the protruding cone out of the ground, Carlo wrapped his hands around the tip and twisted. It turned red and began to throb. He jumped back.

"It shocked me!" he cried.

Slipper pointed to the cone and said, "Look! I think it's throbbing out some kind of message. Is it a beacon?"

"Don't touch it," said Bella who'd been remembering her former neighbor, Henry who'd helped her and Lenny bury that thing in the pit they were planning on using for a root cellar. She'd brought the thing home in the back of the van all the way from New Orleans in a rainstorm. The whole business was a story in itself ... a crazy story she planned to write about some day.

All the neighbors back then were suspicious of Henry – said he was "funny in the head." Cruel stories circulated about Henry being "visited" by "otherworldly beings." Back then "visited" meant getting your butt probed. Henry'd refused to talk about it. And even though neither Bella nor

Lenny had phoned anyone, somehow Henry just showed up with a shovel on his shoulder. Just showed up. They'd been grateful for the help, of course. It took two hours in the pouring rain to bury the stupid thing.

Now 20 some-odd years later, that matt-black contraption was poking up out of the ground. The throbbing light had stopped.

NINE

Bella's had a pressure headache. She sat down on the grass and watched as the kids worked at unearthing the dark metal object. Brain dug the fastest. His curiosity was piqued. A flying bicycle scooter? Hell yeah! Bella had never been a real science buff, but she enjoyed listening when Brain explained wonky things to her as well as practical things like household wiring. She enjoyed hearing his ideas on the reality of time. Back in the day she'd never been all that interested in what Albert Einstein had to say, but when Brain got on a roll exploring Einstein's ideas she got – well, let's be honest – she got a little excited – Mom type excited. Brain made her feel like a little girl again listening to a bedtime story. She loved watching Brain when he got caught up extrapolating Albert Einstein's quantum time theories – out beyond where even the great physicist himself went. Brain's speech mechanisms couldn't keep pace with his ideas. His tongue tripped over his epiglottis allowing saliva and food particles to shoot out from his mouth along with big scientific words.

This same saliva problem which Carlo's mother found endearing were Brain's bête' noir. Kids in grade school made fun of him. His college roommates imitated his saliva drip on YouTube and got over 500 hits.

Carlo was his friend and comforted Brain saying, "Big deal! So, you suffer from an overactive saliva pump! Better than having no saliva at all, right?"

Brain had replied, "Yeah, I guess so. A doctor once told me I have only 68% lip control. The medical terminology is "double dribble suck-back syndrome."

Where Brain's saliva glands were over developed, his self-censoring device was woefully undersized. A typical young man his age scored 56% on the Flickinger scale of self-monitoring ability. Brain scored 12%. Social self-censorship is a brain function most in most folks prevents them from saying things they might regret. Brain scored only 40%. On the other hand, Brain always gave 94% effort on community endeavors like digging up this "thing" in the back yard. Brain gave full gusto to everything in his life. A quick scan of Brain's pcpr (persono-cam-probe-readout) reveals a highly educated young man poorly schooled in social skills – readout of mixed personality traits, 37%. Autistism quotient 33%. Assburgers 30%. Paranoid schizophrenic, 68%. Voice tone; sharp and nasal.

But Brain was generous and actually enjoyed sharing his intelligence. Above all, he knew how to play the cards life had dealt him, especially the brain card where he could help friends with schoolwork. He could provide both a history and a clear explanation of problems; particularly with physics, astral and proto-nuclear. He always found time to tutor his friends for tests. He even taught Grampa Joe to do Facebook and email. And when possible, Brain would sit back in his chair during exams to allow others to see and copy his answers. His memory of psychosexual articles in Self-Zine going back to 2016 is on the order of hypo-prologically legendary.

What Carlo liked most about his friend Brain was listening to Brain's theories about time...

Brain would say, "We have it all wrong. The big Bang did NOT happen a long time ago. It just happened. How do I know this? I know this because the sun is still on fire. The Earth is still molten. The exploding universe just happened. We don't understand this because our time metric is wrong. We are tiny and live on the surface of a planet that is spinning so incredibly fast we can't conceive of the speed at which it's turning. Compound that with our measuring our years in revolutions around the sun. We don't realize it, but we're spinning so fast these billions of years add up quickly. Our problem is we measure time all wrong. The Big bang just happened. Also, every heavenly body began its life around a tiny black hole of intense gravity. These were shot forth during the big bang along with positive matter. Almost immediately each black hole attracted anything and everything around it pulling matter tight and close, melting it all together into a massive molten ball. Hotter and hotter. Only the crust can cool. That's why the universe is on fire!"

"Wow!" was all Carlo could say.

The Hairy Colonizer could handle a shovel as well as Brain. She had been finishing her last semester going for a PHD in bacteriology surviving by maxing out credit cards when she met Carlo and Brain. The Hairy Colonizer had competent animal-like hands unlike any woman Carlo ever met. Hands like fox paws. And she was smart as a weasel. She had facial features like a raccoon with severe bags under her dark grey eyes, a genetic trait from her mother's side. All women in her family had mask-like circles under their eyes. And, of course, a jungle of thick curly wild pubic, under arm, leg and thigh, forearm body hair. And ...I hate to say it, but she had a lot of wiry black chest hair... hence the "Hairy" part in her name. Mean girls in high school claimed she smelled rank, but these were overly sensitive chicks who misunderstood The Hairy Colonizer when she asked if they would volunteer some of their body fluids so she might cultivate body bacteria for her extra Biology class credit. These girls were addicted to Phiso-isohex Super Cleaner and told The Hairy Colonizer she was mistaken about them having bacteria. When she corrected them citing the thirty plus pounds of bacteria colonizing the average human girl at any given moment, the girl called Queenie suggested The Hairy Colonizer should be called 'The Colonizer' from that point on. The name stuck. It was Brain who added 'hairy' because of The Hairy Colonizer 's leg, underarm, and eyebrow hair. He hadn't meant any harm. Fact is, Brain didn't have a mean bone in his skeleton. At a small get together watching a volleyball championship on TV, Someone had asked about Brain's friend, The Hairy Colonizer , wanting to perhaps, date her.

Without thinking Brain had said, "Oh, ... you mean The Hairy Colonizer girl?"

The name stuck.

TEN

Nineteen years ago, Bella's husband Lenny gasped, looked in wonderment skyward, then keeled over dead. One minute he was smiling, laughing, eating supper outdoors. Next minute he was dead. Brain aneurism. It happened almost a year after the night they buried the sky bike. That's what Lenny had called it, a sky bike. At the funeral everyone consoled Bella saying she and Lenny had been such a beautiful couple – the kind you saw in magazines. They had been part of the back-to-the-land movement. She fought back tears remembering Lenny and little Carlo rescuing a goat from the dog pound. Carlo had insisted they save the little guy. They'd been at the pound signing adoption papers for the schnauzer they named George Washingmachine. (because of the dog's spin cycle.) Bella's and Carlo's present dog, Laphonso, had been George Washingmachine's only male pup before they got his spin cycle 'fixed'.

The lady at the adoption desk let it slip they had a goat in the back and the goat's number was up; scheduled to be euthanized the next day. Little Carlo wouldn't allow it – told the lady, "I'll take him. He's my goat now. You can't kill my goat!"

So Lenny and Carlo ended up coaxing the little goat into the van. Carlo carried the puppy. On the ride home Carlo named the goat James Joyce. James Joyce shared Carlo's bed with Rex the cat, and George Washingmachine.

Their van had newspaper-stuffed rust holes above the rear wheel wells; plugs against mosquitoes; a problem as they actually lived in the van for five months after purchasing a burned down old farmstead near Bayou Chein – an hour west of New Orleans. The farm came with the name, Dog Bark Comfort. They got the place dirt-cheap because the original manor house had been struck by lightning more times than folks could remember. All that was left of the main house was charred earth. The barn and chicken coop still stood. An old man called Grampa Joe who'd lived in Bayou Chein all his life said it was called Dog Bark Comfort because years before there'd been another bad fire in the summer kitchen while the family was sleeping. The original log house had burned to the ground. A barking dog woke and saved the occupants. The thing was, those folks hadn't owned a dog.

Bella's father Jim had been a big help after Lenny passed. He'd come down from Maine to clear brush and muck out the old barn. Jim helped everywhere, mended fence to keep the goat in, helped build the outhouse. Unfortunately Bella's father also died – suffered a massive coronary while repairing a stone wall out by the road. In his will Jim stipulated Bella hire a licensed contractor to build a new seven bedroom home on the site of the original Dog Bark Comfort House with seven bedrooms to accommodate all the grandchildren he wanted. Carlo was the only one he got.

Bella's thoughts and memories were like a swarm of bees – darting, stinging her with details from that time – things like the adult-ed evening pottery class at the old high school she and Lenny took. The school got bulldozed in the eighties to make way for a tri-town consolidated school. She and Lenny had made ceramic Christmas presents for everyone on their list. The instructor told Bella she was a natural artist in clay. LESSON ONE – Never tell a hippy girl she's good at anything. She'll latch on and never let go. Besides, Bella had just read an article in Rolling Stone magazine concluding pottery shards would probably be the only remains of human civilization after aliens pan-fried Planet Earth! Might as well be my shards they find, she thought.

Louisiana sunshine streamed into the old chicken coop – the out building Lenny turned into her clay studio – the place where Bella had perfected her craft – where she hand-formed what she called Bella Rosetta icons – modern shards meant to amuse aliens from the planet Stella Europa when they came to visit a dead planet earth.

Bella's memories were skidding again. They fought for traction then caught like snow tires finding dry pavement – caught on what was sticking out of the lawn – this futuristic bicycle she remembered having helicopter-like rotors folded against its sides like beetle wings – this thing she and Lenny and Henry had buried – this thing a bunch of people in a back alley in New Orleans, people who were total strangers, had tossed it into her van twenty years ago.

A strangely unpleasant swamp smell inside her skull accompanied the memories of traveling back to the weird old man riding on the 'thing' when it crashed. And what about the ex-marine who claimed to be a doctor? And, oh God, that special cop, Harold, who'd been chasing the old man?

The mind is not reliable if it has to work hard recalling things it worked so hard to forget – things that happened so many years ago. Sometimes the brain tricks itself. Didn't Freud say the ego constantly lied to its best friend, the id? Residue salts from so many years of potassium shift along neurons, over and over. So much bad cholesterol clogging the old brain. So many dead grey cells which never got properly cleaned up.

Earlier, Brain had set up a nitrogen-cooled solar-powered media-hound device on the bird feeder for on-screen entertainment while they dug. David Bowie's Major Tom and retro music from eighties and 90s was enjoying a popularity re-boot with Carlo's friends. Brain selected a space-rock tune called "Rocket Man" by Elton John to go with the original Star Wars move playing on the hologram screen.

"Hey. Look at this!" shouted Carlo pointing at the screen where the movie had been interrupted by a News Flash featuring The Reverend Al Sharpton who was broadcasting from an early 20th century rustic log building decorated with animal horns – bison, elk, big horn sheep, moose, etc.

"Hey, I know that place … your father and I went there just before you were born, Carlo," said Bella.

"Neat," said Carlo. He liked hearing his mom talk about when his father was alive.

Behind Reverend Al, workmen were busy installing a 10 foot long oak nameplate above the massive oak front door. The freshly lettered name on the plate was spelled out in two-foot tall gold letters, DAVID TCHUMP HALL.

Reverend Al lifted the microphone to his lips, "Sorry for the interruption folks, but our sponsors deem this an important historical event. I'm standing here at what many are calling America's great shame ... the first bankrupt national park. Yes ... it's come to this. Thanks to GOP President Amistad Cruz's budget constraints, congress has demanded we sell off our National Parks for cash needed to bail out First Chase Morgan Bank". Here – watch this...

Here the TV cuts away to Texas Senator Perry. "... and no one even uses these stupid parks. They just sit there doing nothing!"

Back again to Rev. Al ... "The first property being liquidated is the former Yellowstone Park's Great House behind me. Some of you may know it as The Old Faithful Inn. You might not recognize it soon after Mr. Tchump's addition of marble pillars with gold capitals. But that's not why I'm here. As most Americans know, more than a few alien drive-by incidents have occurred in the last few weeks. According to the CDC, contact has occurred – encounters of the third order. Many Americans are frightened. And as we reported yesterday, the number of reported touchings and ... (The Reverend Al confers with an associate then turns to the camera again.) He says that I can say "probings" on the air. The number of probings has spiked. What does this mean to the average American? Well, The new owner here at the park, Mr. David Tchump, the wealthy son of TCHUMP CLOCK WORLD magnate, Hans Banju Tchump, claims he alone will be able to shed new light on these events today. Here he comes now ..."

The doors opened for a short elderly man with a massive but grotesquely twisted jaw who rolled out strapped in his quarter-million-dollar jetto-comfort Laz-E-Porter Bell Boy wheel chair. His shock of golden blond fitch-pomade pompadour hair seemed grotesquely out of place on his pale liver-blotched, wrinkled and warty skull. He wore a loose fitting running suit with a black and white emblem on the chest featuring an Eagle clutching a lightning bolt in one claw and a small rabbit in the other. Obsequious underlings ran up constantly handing him the latest Samsung i-b–a-pad clipboards to thumb-sign.

Tchump smiled a set of sparkling yellow teeth then spoke to Sharpton, "At least I ain't got Alzheimer's ... like my buddy Reagan!"

Tchump then turned to the camera and began, "Okay ... I admit it was my guys plugged up the geyser. Had to do it. You wouldn't believe the crud clogging up that geyser ... hadn't been cleaned since ... well, no one knows. Goddamn thing was spewing absolutely filthy water teeming with *e. coli* I guess, and God knows what else. Bird feces! I could tell you some things about bird feces make your hair stand up. Listen, Al, you know me. I'm not a proud man. I'm not ashamed of my politics. I'm a Reagan conservative... not a Ronald Reagan conservative, a Nancy Reagan conservative."

He started laughing at his own joke until his coughing turned him blue and blood began to trickle down his chin. A flunky whacked him on the back and wiped away the blood.

"There you go, Mr. Tchump."

"Thank you, Nikoli!" Tchump whispered regaining his composure. He continued, "And as God is my co-coconspirator, pure Christian values helped me get where I am today. Will you grant me that much, Al?"

"Please proceed!" said Rev. Al.

"And will you concede that Christian Judeo-Americans are destined to rule the world ... the whole planet?"

"Mr. Tchump. I know you didn't call me and all of America here today to tell us how wonderful America is," said The Reverend Al laughing nervously.

"No no ... You're right. I just get carried away sometimes. I want so much to make America great again. Anyway ... where was I???" mused the old man.

"You were explaining about re-naming the park," whispered Nikoli.

"Okay, Al, you're aware, I'm sure, that I renamed this place Tchump Hall. Listen to me, Al, this place was becoming a real shit hole. Excuse me, but it needed a complete gut-job makeover. I had to sink a lot of money into improvements like granite counter tops, gold plated bathroom fixtures, crown molding, skylights, natural hardwood floors! But of course, there's always going to be complaining shitbag whiners. You know who you are! You people are never happy when a rich man comes along and makes great changes. You know what I'm saying, Al? I didn't get where I am trying to please the folks who kicked my fingers off my bootstraps while I was pulling myself up God's ladder one rung at a time! No sir! Lot of those folks are dead. Nothin to do with me, by the way. And listen to me, Al, if old Ted Turnip and what's his traitor-face girlfriend's name ...Tina Turner? (Nikoli whispers. He waves Nikoli away) ... or any of you libtards out there. Maybe if you hadn't waited around twiddling your thumbs till they found their way up your asses like a bunch of pole-axed sheep. That's what they were doing, Al, while I was plopping down cash to buy this place and the right to name it whatever the Hell I want. And Ted, for what it's worth, you and your shitbag girlfriend could've bought it ...and you could-a named it whatever the Hell YOU wanted. Now listen to me all of you! No one ever called Tchump a soiled sort!"

Here the flunkie whispered in his ear again.

"Okay ... a spoiled sport. Whatever. Point is, I didn't fall off the turnip truck yesterday like in that crazy guy's book that's so popular with young people today. What's the book I'm talking about, Nikoli?"

"An American Broccoli in Key West sir."

"Is that the one where the turnip falls off the truck and then goes around killing everybody?"

"Uh ... yessir."

"As you were saying Mister Tchump ... about the park ..." said Rev. Al.

"Yeah, right. Anyone could have bought this place and named it whatever the Hell they wanted. Could've named it some libtard name like THE PEOPLE'S LODGE FOR AMERICAN WORKERS AND DOPE FIENDS. You could've named it after Martin Luther Kennedy for all I care! How's that for your Roosevelt socialist name? Anyway, what do I know? I'm only one of the richest men in the this the greatest country in the world."

Here he began laughing again ... a belly laugh that ended in another blood-spitting coughing fit stopped only by Nikoli slapping him hard on the back.

Tchump went on, "And you know how I got my wealth, Al?"

"Cheating and bribing?" said Al rolling his eyes.

"Very funny."

"I got it the old fashioned way ... inherited it," said Tchump, "By pulling myself up by my own Goddamned boot straps."

"You were going to tell us why you called you all here today. Let's go. I got other fish to fry," said the Rev. Al with unmitigated annoyance.

"Okay. Listen to me. I called you all here today because it's been brought to my attention that a bunch of aliens been going around probing Americans and God knows who else these ass-monkeys are poking. You're a Christian man, Al! I know you don't approve of that kind of thing. Anyway, I want to get to the bottom of it ... find out why they're here ... and more important HOW the Hell they got here. I want to find out about them – things alike, can they levitate? Can they fly? Are they interested in doing business? Because, guess what! I'm a businessman too. I want to learn from them. I want to know what they know. Scratch my back and I'll scratch yours, Mr. Alien! Hey, if it's money you're after, I'm willing to pay! I'll pay because I want Tchump Industries to be the first company to do business with you aliens.

Listen to me, Al. It's no secret I've had my people trying to contact them. No luck. Maybe my guys' methods aren't so ... how should I say ... kosher? Some of my guys aren't exactly your diplomat types. So far they come up with a big fat zero. Nothing! So, I fired em! Now I'm offering the job to the American people. That's you people out there in TV land – Joe Public! I'm offering one million shares of Clean Air Coal Products as well as one million shares in Tchump Lung and Pancreas Replacement Concepts to the first individual who brings me a living alien willing to sit down and deal. He's got to be alive. You can bring him in a taxi, in a bag ... or in a cage if you like. Whatever floats your goat."

(Tchump was interrupted by Nikoli whispering in his ear)

"That's what I said. I said boat. Whatever. Okay, so... any one of you people out there watching can come waltzing in here, arm in arm with your outer-space alien mother or friend or wife...just married in one of your homosexual chapels! I don't care. Just call before you come. What's our number, Nikoli? "

Nikoli smiled into the camera and handed Tchump a business card.

"Yes. Call this number ... 800 -944-8489. "

ELEVEN

"**H**oly shitbag ... look at this!" shouted Carlo pointing to a flap behind the nose cone. They'd made significant progress on unearthing it.

"Looks like a little door," said the Hairy Colonizer.

"Looks like a gas flap on an older car before the street went electric," said Bear.

Laphonso sniffed around the little door. He was a great sniffer who could follow and find Carlo or Bella up to half an hour after they left the yard just by the smell of their footprints. There was nothing Carlo's dog Laphonso liked more than hanging around with Carlo and "the kids". The mid-size terrier mutt loved humans and he loved to dig. His schnauzer whiskers were designed for tunneling. He was half black lab with a genetically waterproof coat. On walks, Laphonso went out of his way to splash in puddles. An excellent diver he could span seventeen feet airborne off a dock. Unfortunately Laphonso fell in love easily. He was in love with the rabbits in the back yard and he was in love with Bear. He often forgot himself and humped Bear ... who didn't really mind but knew it didn't look good. Laphonso was especially fond of two wild rabbits named Colin Powell and General Patton, who along with hundreds of other wild rabbits, came out evenings to graze in Bella's back yard. No one knew where they came from. One day there were no rabbits; next day there were hundreds.

Laphonso raced up to the edge of the excavation, sniffed, then dashed off to run around the house. He returned to dig and spray fresh dirt rearward through his back legs. Mushroomy soil decay excited him. He searched for a rabbit to hump. He barked. Even when he kicked loose dirt into the hole, Carlo ignored the inconvenience.

"Try opening the flap!" Carlo suggested.

Brain pulled and it opened surprisingly easy exposing an inch thick metal O-ring four inches in diameter.

"Do you suppose that's for towing?" asked Bella.

"... already on it," said The Hairy Colonizer attaching a hardened steel come-along hook while Slipper looped the other end around a tree.

"Ready?" shouted Slipper.

"Go ahead!" said Brain.

Slipper cranked the cable while those in the hole levered the bike back and forth with their shovels until the velocopter-bike was drawn completely out of the dirt and resting on the lawn close to where a certain dog named Pedro had recently done his business – on Laphonsos's territory. This was dog humor.

Who was Pedro?

Pedro was a story unto himself. He was Jimmy Disciple's Chihuahua.

Who was Jimmy Disciple?

Jimmy Disciple was a radio talk-show host who, as we described earlier, had helped Bella forget unpleasant memories. Jimmy Disciple was the surprisingly popular TV show host of Pedro's Pundrity. Jimmy D manipulated Pedro with kibble and other tricks to appear as if the little dog was talking like a living ventriloquist dummy. Pedro's

Pundrity aired every day at five p.m. Before the show these two, man and dog, engaged in some weird behavior. Jimmy D would toss Pedro into his Church-mobile along with a dozen rattling Hav-a-Heart traps. This Church-mobile vehicle was the brainchild of Jimmy Disciple. It was constructed of pastel sticks and wire in the shape of an Easter basket. Jimmy D and Pedro liked to drive around throwing chocolate eggs to children as they headed over to a certain spot near Bella's house where Jimmy D would park, empty his traps in Bella's yard, and wait while Pedro did his business, both #1 and #2. This was usually around noon. The little dog would hold it for days at a time if he needed, until arriving in Bella's yard.

What was Jimmy D releasing from those Hav-a-Heart traps?

Rabbits!

Jimmy Disciple lived in what some Holy Rollers called Southern sin with his Injustani boyfriend, Colonel Steve Golub-Singh. For propriety's sake they insisted they were not a gay couple. Just ... you know, "roommates." And FYI, Jimmy D did not drive regularly to Bella's yard just for Pedro's sake. He came because of a problem resulting from Colonel Steve Golub-Singh's ... how shall we put this? His PTSD driven emotional instability? This presented as bi-polar behavior, which when manic, trumped The Colonel's better judgment. After Googling the symptoms Jimmy D home-diagnosed his partner as having assburgers syndrome as well. And Jimmy D would be the first to admit that he just liked the way it sounded; assburgers – like some kind of obscene fast food. And in any domestic argument with Colonel Steve, Jimmy would simply say, "Well, there you go again. That's your assburgers acting up!"

Calling the Colonel an assburger gave Jimmy D power over his lover. When The Colonel asked for serious evidence about his condition, Jimmy D only needed to remind The Colonel of the time he responded to an ad run by a local rabbit rescue center. The Colonel had been in one of his manic states when he adopted the cuddly Easter bunny couple – symbols of Jesus and Mary, ostensibly gifts for Jimmy D's Church of the Blessed Acolyte. So, why, Jimmy D asked, did the Colonel insist on feathering a little nest for the bunnies in their conjugal love bed...up by his pillow, and then naming them Colin Powell and George Patton? And why did The Colonel relegate Pedro's nest to down on the floor by their feet where his tail got stepped on more than once? Was that not just one more passive aggressive assburger symptom?

The rabbit general duo was dragged out of their cage to appear with Pedro in an Easter basket that April on Jimmy's TV ministry show. More than a few viewers, especially the born agains, liked the little "manger scene" Jimmy assembled that December where Jimmy Disciple dressed Pedro as Joseph and dressed the bunnies as Mary and the holy infant. Viewers loved the sweet bunny Wise Men and sent in their checks, for thousands. But there were others who were upset complaining the Easter eggs, which the Colonel insisted on dyeing olive green camo, looked like hand grenades.

The Colonel maintained that he'd originally bought the bunnies to provide amusement and company for Pedro. Jimmy D agreed the little dog did demand a ton of attention.

Now, all of this would have meant nothing had The Colonel not assumed the rabbit couple had been 'fixed' simply because the procedure was listed on the bill under 'fees' for which he'd paid cash money at the rescue center. Regardless, somehow it had not been done. This resulted in a sudden rabbit population explosion. And, though he had no hard evidence, The Colonel suspected Pedro had a hand in the rabbits escaping and now living underneath the house.

That should have been the end of it, but it wasn't. Their house had been built on top of a series of honeycombed rock tunnels from which a geological aneurysm allowed the slow release of inner-earth hydro-pyride gas – a natural aphrodisiac, small amounts of which turned the now feral rabbits into aggressive super breeders. Within a year their yard ('Compound Commando' as the Colonel called it) was over-run. The Colonel was by then walking the compound perimeter naked at night, hiding in the bushes whenever someone passed on the sidewalk. He was the one who discovered the yard was overrun with inbred rabbits, rabbits who exhibited five legged offspring as well as really stupid buck toothed bunnies. In fact, it was one of these super-wrinkled buck-toothed bunnies labeled Rudold Googliani who went viral as a sick Facebook joke. There was even a one-eared bunny, which Jimmy D featured on his TV show – for only one week after a noticeable decrease in checks.

This honeycombed earth made an ideal warren for the geometrically expanding rabbit clan. Some say Colonel Steve and Jimmy D overreacted when they purchased and deployed two dozen Hav-a-Heart traps to catch as many feral rabbits as they could. Colonel Steve Golub-Singh began referring to the rabbits as 'gooks' or 'VC' while Jimmy D called them "supplicants." After catching a gook, while still inside the trap, Colonel Steve spray-painted each bunny's back in a military camouflage pattern before releasing them in neighborhoods near enough to drive to easily but far enough that the supplicants didn't come back. The camo marking identified them if they returned and helped determine just how far away they needed to be dumped. Bella's street turned out to be the red line. Her grassy yard was ground zero for dumping rabbits as well as Pedro's favorite poop site. How easily a daily ritual is established … catch, spray paint, release, poop.

Laphonso was a good dog – a reasonable dog. He was not territorial. Though he disapproved having to tiptoe around Pedro's droppings, Laphonso was fond of small dogs like Pedro and would hump the little fellow whenever they happened to meet on Bella's lawn. This humping upset Jimmy D even though Pedro didn't mind. It seemed so anti-Jesus. Humping was one of many ways Laphonso showed affection. He had learned the hard way that humping a human was frowned upon. Pedro joined in humping rabbits when he had the opportunity. Laphonso tended to get lightheaded when licking a bunny's soft lagomorphic cheeks and usually didn't stop until he'd swallowed the bunny's ears right down to the bunny's eyeballs, which were, more often than not, rolling in pleasure.

TWELVE

The ancients say thunder is God's angry voice. Take cover! Clouds just love to mess things up. Storms like to slide out of nowhere on beautiful days. The kids finished unearthing the velocopter-bike just before three angry purple clouds released their fury. It rained hard for two minutes then stopped. The sun came out.

Pedro and Jimmy D had driven up in the church-mobile hauling seventeen Hav-a-Heart traps filled with rabbits. They'd waited for the rain to stop before quietly emptying the traps. Pedro was getting ready to perform his daily ablutions under an Australian pine in a shaded corner of Bella's yard when Jimmy D saw the kids resume digging. He watched patiently for the kids to haul out the velocopter. They set the odd contraption on the lawn. Though he'd never actually seen one, Jimmy D knew what this was. All his life he'd been a fan of Spacey-Steve and the Dudester-Boy Comic books. Every fan and collector was familiar with the velocopter, which first appeared in Comic #6 and again in book numbers 7, 8, 9, and 22. Velocopter-bikes were the preferred method of short distance transport on planet Triburistan. Ray Bradbury also featured these acrobatic velocopter arial bikes in some of his best stories illustrated by Coleen Doran. Jimmy Disciple watched while his brain put two and two together ... (1) Tchump's offering big bucks for an alien interview ... and (2) If this thing turned out to really be an alien velocopter IT JUST MIGHT BE AN ALIEN MAGNET!

Jimmy D's steel trap mind extrapolated to ... "Show me the money, baby!"

Jimmy D also knew that he was not alone in this velocopter knowledge. He knew anyone else happening along might come to the same conclusion. He had to work fast.

Leaving his emptied traps he popped out from behind the tree where he'd been watching and said, "Hey guys, wassup? ... Hello, ma'am."

He did not say hello to Bear because protocol does not require greeting a CareBear© though some will exchange pleasantries with AI devices anyway.

Jimmy D bowed slightly and smiled at Grampa Joe saying, "Hello, sir!"

Grampa Joe did not return the smile but lowered the barrel of his shotgun which he'd instinctively aimed at the man with the full head of blond Jesus hair and the Van Dyke beard. Grampa Joe had the rifle with him because he sometimes "harvested" a rabbit or two. He had a taste for rabbit pie. (like chicken pot pie, but tastier).

"Please allow me to introduce myself. My name is Jimmy ... Jimmy Disciple ... friends call me Jimmy D. And this little feller here is my dog, Pedro."

Bear looked uneasy.

Bella's face brightened. She recognized the TV personality's golden hair and the snow-white sparkling teeth. She said, "I think I know who you are. I listen to your show every day ... Pedro's Punditry, right? And Pedro! You really are such a sweet little dog. You know, Mr. Disciple, your show has helped me through some of my darkest times."

Jimmy D pressed Bella's hand to his rubbery lips in a gentlemanly kiss. Jimmy D pinched Pedro reminding him this would not be a good time to get one of his shiny red boners.

"It's always a pleasure meeting my listeners ... and are these lovely children yours?" asked Jimmy D.

"Oh Lord, no. Only this one here, my Carlo. These are his friends, Slipper, The Hairy colonizer, and Brain!" said Bella squeezing Carlo's hand.

"Nice to meet you folks," said Jimmy D. "I hope I'm not disturbing you. Me and Pedro, we were just walking by and, well, we couldn't help wondering what you are doing with this contraption you have here. What is it?"

Carlo responded, "We don't exactly know, sir ... maybe some kind of motor scooter that my Mom and Dad buried a few years back."

"Now, why would you ...? Anyway, you know, this is the kind of thing that's right up my alley. Me and Pedro here just love to tinker with junk like this ... don't we Pedro? We're actually thinking of launching a new show called GREAT JUNK."

Pedro blinked. His penis was beginning to lengthen. It was cherry red.

Slipper looked at it with alarm.

"You wouldn't be interested in selling it, would you?" asked Jimmy D.

Carlo looked at his friends with surprise and said, "Gee, I don't know. We kinda just dug it up ... hadn't really given it any thought ... we ... just ..."

"How about this? Let's say I offered ... oh say ... thirty-five bucks? I think that's a fair price," said Jimmy Disciple flashing his best smile – the smile he used when convincing old folks to write him checks.

Carlo massaged his chin. He'd not been expecting this.

"Okay, look ... I'll go up to $200! That's the best I can do. And I think that's a fair offer," said Jimmy D.

Bella could see Brain pumping his fist mouthing the words "YES! Take the money, Carlo!"

The Hairy Colonizer and Slipper also were grinning and nodding their heads enthusiastically. But Bear nudged Carlo and whispered he should maybe wait. Bear instinctively didn't trust the man.

"What do you think, Mom?" asked Carlo.

"You kids did all the work. It's up to you," said Bella.

The Hairy Colonizer said, "Carlo ... let's sell it. I mean ... bird in the hand and all that. And since we've all been, like, working ... digging together ... shouldn't we decide together?"

"Can you give us a minute, sir?" asked Carlo.

"Sure, sure!" said Jimmy D walking Pedro to the end of the lawn behind a gumbo limbo tree where Pedro arched his back and clenched his teeth in concentration. His business had been interrupted earlier. By the time Pedro did his business and Jimmy D came back he found Slipper on her call-pen to TCHUMP CLOCK WORLD headquarters.

She said, "We just want to just check this out with the Tchump people ... just to make sure Tchump won't give us any of that alien money reward for it,"

This surprised Jimmy D. Did these moron kids suspect they had something valuable here? Jimmy D got nervous ... but he tried to keep his cool.

Slipper held a hand up to shush them. She began talking, "Yes. Hello. My name is Slipper and I'd like to speak to Mr. Tchump? ... not Flipper ... it's Slipper ... S ... l ... i ... p ... p ... e ... r. That's right. Yes, that's my real name ... No ... uh, no, I don't have a call permission number ... but I do have a ... what? Well, how do I get ... a ... HELLO! HELLO!
"

The Hairy Colonizer grabbed the pen-speak from Slipper and shouted into it, "Listen you little nail-polished functionary ...no dirty pickle Mother fried willie-witch bitch hangs up on us! ... Hello?"

Click.

"She hung up on me! Can you believe that?" said The Hairy Colonizer.

"I can. Happens to me all the time," said Jimmy Disciple in a way that was hard to interpret, "That's how some people operate."

Brain grabbed the pen-call and hit re-dial, "Here let me try. You just have to pretend you speak their language ... (he began speaking with a Dutch accent) Hello ... vell, yes, dish here ish da Prezident of Shell oil company callink witch some goot newts for Meester Tchump! Well, don't be too lonk pecaudze I'm a very bishy man!"

Holding his hand over the mouthpiece Brain whispered... "She's reaffirming me! ... (back into the device). Oh yes ... Dis is Otto Crankshafter ... And I ... what? No I din't vant the cafeteria ... What did I want? Vell, I vanted to know if there would be any money ... or reward from Mr.

Tchump ... for what we think might be a UFO spacecraft? ... Yes I do unnerstant English ... Yes, I am very much aware that there is difference between za alien and za spaceship bicycle ... but I ..."

Click.

She hung up on me," said Brain, looking perplexed.

Carlo turned to Jimmy Disciple and said, "Will you go two fifty?"

Jimmy Disciple smiled and wrote out a rubber check for two hundred fifty dollars drawn on The Chinese Jesus Bank of The Universal Bit-Coin.

"Well, it was a real pleasure meeting you folks," said Jimmy D. And turning his smile on Bella, said, "It's not every day a man meets such a pretty lady."

Bear looked uneasy.

THIRTEEN

Having made the deal, Bella, Carlo, Brain, Slipper, Bear, and the Hairy Colonizer, together with Jimmy Disciple, tried but could not muscle Jimmy D's recent purchase up into Jimmy D's Churchmobile. It kept getting hung up on empty Hav-a-Heart traps. It was as if the velocopter had a mind of its own, and that mind-set was determined the artifact would stay where it was.

On the front of his Churchmobile, Jimmy D had wired small bubbling lights inside a Christmas wreath. It looked oddly like a whaling ship's figurehead. What made it extra-special were four-foot angel wings attached to each of the rear doors. Then, Jimmy D cried out. He'd pulled a muscle in his lower back while struggling with the velocopter-bike and lay moaning on the grass. Pedro and Laphonso licked his face. He did the smart thing, though. He gave up and left the machine where it was. He did, however, give Carlo and his friends an additional $10 to cover it with a tarp and some leaves to hide it from prying eyes.

When Bella offered Jimmy D coffee and some ibuprofen he politely refused. He was late for his daily broadcast of Pedro's Punditry. Saying goodbye he promised that when he went live in half an hour he'd give a special wink into the cam-a-vid for Bella.

FOURTEEN

Jimmy Disciple limped up the front steps of his house Pedro in one hand and holding his back with the other. He tossed Pedro onto the couch and ladled out a bowl of low-cal steak-ums for the Chihuahua. Because his back hurt to bend down he set the bowl on the couch. From his closet he fetched a white, red, and gold-piped Elvis-Jesus robe and threw it over his shoulders. He groaned with every move. He was late. Jimmy hated being late. He splashed mink oil on his hands, rubbed them vigorously in his lovely blond Jesus hair before fingering it back like Billy Graham. He mugged sideways, left, and then right in his *way-too-expensive* electro-magnet mercury-silver halide obsequiator complimenting makeup mirror© hoping to coax from it at least a little compliment. This latest concession to vanity flattered the owner's image. But that image had to satisfy certain pre-programmed criteria determined by a committee of cloned Joan Rivers bitch-slappers.

Nothing from the mirror yet.

Jimmy D grabbed his favorite hairbrush – the bunny boar bristle brush Colonel Steve Sing made for him on his birthday from whiskers yanked out of the cheeks of trapped rabbits. Jimmy D dabbed dusty rouge on his cheeks. At least the stupid rabbits were good for something. He turned sideways fluttering his fatuous flamingo TV smile. Because of his back pain it took longer than usual, but finally the obsequiator mirror squeaked out a so-so purr of approval. It then paid the following back-handed compliment, "Well, you don't look as sickly as you did before slopping on your makeup."

"That's all I get?" Jimmy whined.

"Okay asshoul, how about this? You're beautiful ... beautiful as the noble melting face of the Queen of Chernobyl. Jesus Christ, that's the best you're going to get, sweetheart!" croaked the mirror registering barely a 20% on the enthusiasm meter.

Unhappy with the compliment but not wanting to get into a pissing match with his mirror, Jimmy D carefully slung his un-tuned guitar over his shoulder. But he tweaked his back again. He groaned.

"Jesus Christ ... somebody gimme a Goddamned Ibudextrin!" he muttered to his own image in the compliment mirror. Okay, sure, the mirror was having its own problems and was under no obligation to help ease his psychological and physical pain. And he really had no intentions of getting physical with the way too expensive electro-magnet mercury-silver halide obsequiator complimenting mirror. But when the damn thing muttered a barely audible, "Ugly asshole", at Jimmy's back as he was leaving the bathroom, Jimmy D lost it. He punched the stupid mirror. Jimmy watched his own reflection shatter. As it splintered into the sink the mirror tried to talk ... tried to compliment, but its voice was broken.

"Oh Christ!" said Jimmy fumbling one of the little gold colored pills out of a pocket in his Elvis jacket. He popped it dry onto his tongue and half chewed half swallowed it by the time he shuffled his feet onto the X mark painted on the floor of his studio. He shimmied his shoulders as best he could positioning himself in front of the automatic camera. He sighed and relaxed, took a deep breath feeling the lovely heat of sixteen LED Hot-God spots bathing him in a soft heavenly glow. Settling his robe more comfortably on his shoulders with another shimmy-hitch, something he'd picked up watching Elvis tapes, he pressed down on the red floor switch, mouthed the countdown. And a 5 ... and a 4 ... and a 3 ... and a 2 ... and a 1. The red light flashed. Wait for it ... wait for it! Then he was on-air-live. He watched his halo glow in the monitor as he launched into his daily sermon opening his heart and soul to the universe over the worldwide worm-wire super-special channel for spiritual believers.

Jimmy Disciple began crooning the soft Jesus porn-hymn he'd written himself –"God, you make me hard! God you kill me with your love!"

Closing his eyes and rocking his head side to side he tapped his foot to the guitar's twang. Triple reverb back feed. Picking up steam he sang, "Lord, you got me by the balls. I'm a strummin' and a-swayin'. Kiss me Lord, you give me power for fukk-rock staying! I will love you Lord until you cum. Because for me, Lord, you the only one! Amen motherfukkr amen!"

The Ibudextrin kicked in then with a caffeine after-burst. He began gyrating wildly. His face practically touched the lens as he became a sweating wrinkled moaning ecstasy monster – something ripped from a Hans Bruegel painting. He began punching out ad-libbed lyrics, something he was famously popular for, "It's a one fo' da money ... too far da show ... free da cat fat Freddy ... Now blow cat, blow! Now don't chew! Jes' swallow my socks. I sukk on yer box, Yeah, you sure can do everything, but don cum on my potato-latke jew fried news! Oh, you can do anything, as long as you love'n those goose-snake blues!"

The backache was gone. He could see his phone register lights blinking with every called-in pledge. He was killing it, raking in the pledges ... ten, fifteen, thirty five dollars a pop!

Six years ago when he'd first aired this show offering himself as just one more country western Elvis wannabe, he would try and try to remember and sing the correct words. But he'd stumble and hit sour chords. Sometimes he'd go back to the beginning and start over. A debacle. He had no listenership.

But that was before he became Jimmy Disciple. And now with new laws enabling him to incorporate as Jimmy Disciple, he was allowed to just make up lyrics fresh every day ... or he could just hum while rolling his eyes in religious miasma. Sometimes he talked smut in tongues while making it look like Pedro had the potty mouth. It was all legal now that he'd incorporated. It was now legal to make it seem like the little dog was singing, keening that high whine until Pedro's surprisingly large lipstick red wanker would come flopping out wagging side to side. And, of course, everything changed for the better when he discovered how a few ibudex pills on the tongue could help a singer/preacher drift out over TV La La Land like some strato-nimbus soft porno cloud.

Smiling like The Pressure Cat, Jimmy turned toward the camera joining Pedro in sweet harmony. This was not fake but something that happened organically. It was a beautiful and natural thing when they wailed together – like coyotes howling at the moon with their naked inner Jesus hanging out for all the world to see.

Now he was in a groove. And thinking how much he loved Jesus, Jimmy D. thrust his face forward and delivered his daily sermon ...

"And a big hello out there to all my dear dear friends! Is everybody ready? Everybody got their defribulators taped under their units? Gocher catch-bowls and towels ready? Thennnnnnnnnnnn fire em up and shake 'em if you got em, cause we're gonna fly and cry and git ourselves off with a load of Jimmy's twistin' love spectacular."

Here Jimmy threw his guitar onto the bed in the corner and despite his back issue, began a hip-shoulder-ass gyration dance, a series of wrenching grinding thrusts that had made him a household name and a favorite with the ladies ... a dance designed to make Yo-Mama wet her panties and make Daddy's dildo squeal for oil like some hot-spanked rubber monkey.

"Yeahhhhh! It's Jimmy D coming at you from right here in filthy God's Town U.S.A. Me and Pedro coming live to tell you that we love the crap out of each and every one of you and all your friends and your family. And let's not forget all our little doggie friends either."

Here Jimmy snatched up Pedro and held him an inch from the camera so that his wanker might brush against the lens. Pedro, having been plied all his life with kibble was into it. For five spectacular minutes the little dog flashed the most endearing facial expressions ending with a curious and now world famous gummy smile while continuing to waggle that famous, larger-than-life, fiery red erect penis. All the while an electric ticker tape begging for donations scrolled across the bottom of each viewer's TV screen. And the checks poured in ... mostly made out to Pedro. Jimmy'd had to add the name of Pedro of Eternal Lightness Church to his checking account.

After fifteen minutes of filthy-but-good jokes, mostly at Pedro's expense, repeating encounters with a fictitious large-breasted Mexican lady, an exchange of casserole recipes, some bad luck stories where a chump gets made well again by a personal Jesus intervention, and some local gossip complete with photos and/or video, Jimmy D headed the show down into its runway glide-path landing with ... "Friends I want to end today's show on a serious note if that's alright with you. You see ... there's been a lot of talk lately about creatures and aliens observing us. But I ask you ... do we care? My answer and Pedro's answer is ... (Here Jimmy D held the little dog up to the camera while squeezing his tail which was Pedro's cue for opening his mouth while Jimmy D ventriloquized the word) "No."

"That's right Pedro. No! No no no no no! Why? Because Jesus is our Loving Savior and is always watching over us. And when it comes right down to it He's the only one we care about. Oh yes, my friends, we ARE under the watchful eye of Jesus. Now ... I may be going out on a limb here, but I feel confident telling you right now that these aliens may be coming to visit me and Pedro soon! Why? Because they understand this wonderful magical dog here is a conduit of universal love. And by the way, Pedro wants me to ask you for a solid. These aliens have suggested by their actions and by the messages they have sent to this little dog here ... that they want you to send them your personal note of reassurance ... any little contribution you can afford. Okay then, looks like we just about out of minutes ... just enough time for ... Pedro's Punditry!"

With his hand hidden by his Elvis robe, Jimmy Disciple shoved a mini-chunk of bitter-root into the dog's back door making the Jack Russell/Chihuahua chirp and work his jaw as if speaking while Jimmy D said with unmoving lips ... "So long humans ... Don't forget Pedro loves you. And please don't forget that our good work with paralyzed children would not be possible without your generous donations. From the bottom of my little doggie heart, Muchos Thankos and Mios Dios Russell Rancheros! God Bless and goodbye! And a special hello to our new friends out there, Bella and her wonderful children!"

FIFTEEN

Slipper, The Hairy Colonizer, Carlo, Brain and Grampa Joe enjoyed walking Laphonso. He was such a good dog. Where a lot of dogs chase rabbits, Laphonso was content to smooch and lick a bunny. Bella could look out any night around six thirty and see twenty or thirty big hares grazing on the lawn, playing with Laphonso, gamboling, snoozing together while Laphonso deep throated their ears. Though it left their ear fur saliva-covered they didn't seem to mind.

"If they don't mind, I don't mind," sighed Bella. As long as he doesn't do it to me or the girls."

Bella refused to get Laphonso fixed.

Walking Laphonso together gave Slipper and The Hairy Colonizer the opportunity for girl chats.

On one such walk Slipper said, "I'm not the kind of girl who cares what people think. You know that, right?"

"Yeah ... no ... I mean, a girl's got to be her own person," agreed The Hairy Colonizer.

Slipper said, "I mean, that's probably why a lot of the guys don't call me. And not everybody knows I'm not with Herr Art Wolf any more. And there's this guy, Thomas Keenan, who tells everybody I'm gay just because I won't go out with him. I mean the dude's got gross hair growing all over his back. It's like a pelt, like some wild pig that got bit by a werewolf or something. He kept asking why I won't date him ... so I told him and guess what!"

"He gets all huffy, right?"

"Yeah. Then he says "real" women dig a hairy man. I said, "Dude, if you can't take the truth, don't ask for oatmeal, right?"

The Hairy Colonizer replied, "For sure. I mean, a girl's got to be herself. Otherwise, it's a slip and a fall on the slide toward being somebody else. Then what's she got?"

The Hairy Colonizer replied, "You are so right-on, little Bitch sister. You're one strong lady – someone who can stand up for herself! Men are such control freak know-it-alls. Don't tell anybody this, but the only guy I'm even a little bit attracted to is bi. Truth is, I wasn't really all that attracted to Herr Art Wolf. He had this weird raw meat animal smell when he took his clothes off. I tried to like his stink, but the chemistry was wrong ... like a three out of 40. Don't tell anybody this, but the guy shaves his pubes. He does it because his pubes grow to be like two feet long. So he shaves. Now he's like a Ken Doll down there. I don't know what's worse.

"So ... what DID you like about him?" asked The Hairy Colonizer, "I mean, you went out with the guy for over a year."

"Well ... I think I fell in love with his name and then hoped the feeling would generalize into love if he kissed and squeezed me enough. But I was the one ended up having to do all the kissing and squeezing. Then he started fishing for compliments about his package ... wanted me to tell him he had the biggest dorkal unit I'd ever seen. Why do men want to hear that crap? They're all the same down there. Kinda ugly if you ask me. Maybe an inch difference. I can't tell. As long as it doesn't hurt. Anyway, the love thing didn't happen.

And then little things started to bother me, little things that attracted me at first started to repel me."

"Like what??"

"Like ... the way he walked."

"The way he walked?"

"Yeah. It was more like he loped. And he expected me to lope along with him. We'd never just go for a walk. We'd go for a lope."

"What else?"

"I can't think of anything right off ... wait ... there was this thing he had for ground lamb. He'd eat it raw right off the Styrofoam packet it came in. No fork. Just bend his head down and scarf it up with his teeth. Gross."

"So what do you like about the bi-guy?"

"I like that he's polite. Nice dresser. Eats with a fork. Not afraid to talk about his feelings. But, see ... I couldn't get hot for having sex with him--no electric zing from caressing his body. He's got slender arms and this delicate neck. On the positive side he's got sweet facial features. You know what I want?"

"What?"

"I want a surfer dude – some guy with tanned arms all covered with beautiful fine blond forearm hairs. I want to touch and smell his arm hairs and lick his muscles. Men's forearms can have this nutty hot toasty smell if they've been out in the sun."

"Did your bi-guy's forearms smell?"

"Not really. If there was any odor he covered it up with "hunk-man" truck cologne. He tried. Got to give him that much. No. I'll admit, I'm a hoe for a chiseled guy. I get turned on stroking and petting guy's abs ... maybe patting his ass. Don't care all that much about his cock. Pretty ugly. Not that my twat's all that gorgeous. I do love looking at a mans' ass though...you know, squeezing his buns!" Slipper said.

"Me too," said the Hairy Colonizer.

"Can I tell you something personal?"

"Yeah, you can!"

"I masturbate all the time," Slipper whispered.

"Me too!" smiled the Hairy Colonizer, "Give me a three-speed vibrator and I'm off to the races. Sometimes I'll do it for an hour!"

"Sometimes I think I might be out of control," said Slipper.

"Why do you say that?"

"Because I do it a lot ... like I once counted forty times in one day!"

"Wow! Your vibrator must be really great. Is it gentle?"

"Really gentle. But it's got like, hyperspeed too. And it's cute. It's really old. It's like a father figure to me. It's called the butterfly kiss. This thing is so old it's got a freaking wall plug! No batteries or Wi-Fi. They made the Butterfly Kiss back when America still made stuff – Made in Dayton Ohio back in the Fifties."

"Could I borrow it sometime? I'll clean it afterward."

"Sure. You can borrow it if you want. Let me ask you something though ..."

"Shoot." Said The Hairy Colonizer.

"My Butterfly Kiss is a machine, I know that, but it's kind of become my boyfriend. Is it possible to fall in love with your vibrator? Seriously."

"I guess so. Yeah, for sure now that I think about it. I think most girls are in love with their vibrators not just because they're so good at what they do, but because they're not always TELLING US WHAT TO DO. You know what I'm saying?"

"Hello! Yeah! And guess what!" asked Slipper.

"What?" asked The Hairy Colonizer.

"I tried letting my bi-guy operate my Butterfly Kiss on me."

"How'd that go?"

"Disaster. Like doing a three way where NOBODY gets off. Nothing happened. But as soon as he left and it was just me and Madame Butterfly... two minutes and, BINGO I'm in La La Land!"

"What about relationships?" asked The Hairy Colonizer .

"Oh yeah, I like the whole relationship thing alright. And that's what's good about me and my bi guy. In a perfect world I'd live with Bi guy, but I'd have sex and kids with Mr. Blond Forearm Horse-Cock."

"That'd be great for a while, but I bet in six months you'd be thinking about the Butterfly Kiss," said The Hairy Colonizer .

"I like sweet talk," said Slipper.

"Oh yeah. For sure. If a guy calls me pretty I'll let him boink me. Simple as that," said The Hairy Colonizer .

"Okay, you know what I hate?" asked Slipper.

"What?" asked The Hairy Colonizer.

"When the guy's all hot to trot ... got this huge stiffie...it's throbbing inside his pants. So big he can't hide it ... and then, just when I need to hear the tiniest eensieweensie compliment. Some meaningless little compliment's all I want ... he won't deliver. He knows I want it. Won't give it. And it's not like I'm asking for a declaration of love forever because I'm more beautiful than princess Snow White. Just ... maybe ... you have pretty eyes. Something like that," said Slipper.

"You hit the nail right on the head there sister. You hate having to ASK him, don't you?" said The Hairy Colonizer .

"Right. Just to let him know what I'm looking for I'll ask him if he's had any, you know, nice thoughts about me. Oh boy. You think I asked if he ever had sex with his mother. He'll start flopping around all nervous trying to think of something, and all he can come up with is some lame old cliché' like, "Yeah, I was just thinking what a nice person you are!" said Slipper.

"Right. The freaking NICE PERSON bullshit," agreed The Hairy Colonizer, "I've heard that one."

"Really? That's the best you can come up with, Douchebag? No way! No boink for you tonight!" said Slipper.

"Right, No boinkey boink."

"But you know what I just love?" said Slipper.

"What?" asked The Colonizer.

"You're going to say I'm crazy, but I just love it when a guy tells me ... and you're going to hate this. I just love when a guy tells me he loves me. Okay, I know it's sappy and stupid. And of course I know he probably doesn't really mean it. At least I hope he doesn't mean it. But ohhhhh I just get all gooey wet and slimy-stupid when a guy whispers the L-word. I mean, seriously, my hips start gyrating that shimmy slip-dancing routine and I just want to kiss the nearest erect pole or hug some warm muscle with hair on it. You ever feel like that?" asked Slipper.

"Hello! Am I a piece of dirt? Of course I like hearing the L-word! And, like you just said, the guy doesn't really have to mean it! And I'll cut the guy some slack because he's all excited from crawling all over me and probably does think he might probably love me ... at least for the moment. I don't care that his love is some primal monkey emotion. At least it's an emotion. That's something for a guy. See, I know in my heart that when he's about to explode his urgent sperm backed-up lust, he thinks he truly loves me from the bottom of his scrotum ... loves me because he knows I'm the one creature other than his Bo Bo Doll with that's going to squeeze the cum out of his Buji stick into my hot wet slimy soft and heavenly possum," said The Hairy Colonizer."

They both laughed.

"Hey, what's Laphonso doing? Is that another rabbit he's got in his mouth? He's not ... ?"

"Oh yes he is!"

"Is that gross, or what?" asked Slipper.

The Hairy Colonizer said, "You and I might think it's gross, but he's a dog and he's just doing what his dog bacteria is telling him to do."

"You're really into all that bacteria stuff, aren't you!" said Slipper.

"Yeah. You know they're finding out now that bacteria is behind every living creature's behavior ... including Laphonso's. I just read this article by Erin Adley of the *San Francisco Gate*. This lady makes everything about bacteria fit together like a cardboard puzzle with a thousand interlocking parts. It's like someone placed each puzzle piece in the spot next to where it's supposed to go ... but didn't finish doing the final step of interlocking them all ... just laid them close to where they're supposed to go ... half an inch of space between all thousand or so pieces. Then when the bell goes off in Erin's head ... she just snaps them all together. BAM! That's how if feels when I think about bacteria. All those pieces fitting together like magic. There's always something new being discovered in the bacteria world ... like recently this guy David Relman wrote that together, all of the bacteria in our body would be the size and weight of a large liver. He says the microbiome behaves like any other organ in the human body. See, our bodies have their own unique microbiome, cultivated from birth and built from our genes and diet and are nurtured by exposure to ... say ... the family dog (They both glanced at Laphonso) ... and from dirt we ate out of the sandbox as kids ... or the antibiotics we took for ear infections."

"Must be great to be a scientist," mused Slipper.

"It is! Understanding bacteria is like space exploration or studying the oceans. That's what this lady, Dr. Julie Parsonnet says. She's this Stanford epidemiologist who calls her peers, "microbonauts." She's studying how the micro biome influences weight gain and obesity by adopting new diets which alter micro biomes, which in turn alter the way we digest food or process energy from it. It might even affect and change the foods we crave. And get this ... at least one parasite – toxoplasmosis gondi – reproduces only in cats. There are these studies which show when mice or rats are infected with the parasite, it makes them less afraid of cats, and therefore, more likely to be eaten by cats who will shit out the eggs for more parasites. How cool is that?"

(Taken from an article by Erin Adley, San Francisco - *SFGate*)

SIXTEEN

To relieve tension in her neck and shoulders The Hairy Colonizer learned a yoga move on Youtube where you grasp your jaw firmly in your right hand and apply a quick jerk to with your left hand which is holding the top of your head ... add a little twist and ... pop! A pleasant burning sensation is followed by relief.

The Hairy Colonizer could be in the middle of a conversation or alone. Slipper once counted her doing twenty-four neck pops in three hours. This ligament popping made Slipper uneasy and Bella nauseous. But it was so much a part of The Hairy Colonizer's behavior that she was no longer aware she did it. Just pop, pop, pop. So much of The Hairy Colonizer 's behavior was unconscious. Like, when Slipper asked her if she was a control freak she looked at her friend oddly as if she'd been accused of child abuse.

Even when Carlo pointed out to Miss Hairy Colonizer it was unusual that she consistently beat boys wrestling, pinning them easily. She said, "So what! Some girls are good at gymnastics. Some play soccer. I happen to be good at wrestling. It's because my father was a wrestling coach. He taught me how to protect myself.

How often had Carlo videoed The Hairy Colonizer placing men in painful arm bar holds. After breaking an aggressive date's elbow she started getting a bad reputation. But that only made guys want to challenge her.

Her ability to control men physically led to some calling her a 'control freak'. She suggested they might be confusing 'control freak' with "highly motivated woman." Her high school biology teacher had written "highly motivated" in red ink on her report card after the class spent a week studying bacteria. That was the beginning of her love affair with the world of tiny bugs.

When Brain first called Janis "The Colonizer" he was noting similarities in the manner The Hairy Colonizer formed controlling relationships with men and the manner in which bacteria formed colonies. Brain was simply saying that when The Hairy Colonizer felt comfortable with a guy she moved inside his system, colonizing him and taking over control of his brain like bacteria might colonize an intestine. "Hairy" got added to Janis's name of "The Colonizer" when Slipper was identifying her to a mutual friend. This friend had said, "I'm not sure who you're talking about." Slipper answered – "Janis – The hairy one! You know. The one who doesn't shave her pits or legs or bush – The Hairy Colonizer!

As Slipper and The Hairy Colonizer walked Laphonso The Hairy Colonizer asked, "I mean, like, am I crazy for wanting to have a real say-so in my relationships with guys?"

Slipper replied, "No."

The Hairy Colonizer replied, "Thank you!"

"But, you have to admit you haven't had a relationship with a man in a long time. And I'm just saying that might be because you insist on you know, colonizing your males," joked Slipper.

"No ... but I'm just saying," said The Hairy Colonizer, " that if I did have a guy, shouldn't I have just as much right to be the one to determine where our life is headed and who's driving?"

"For sure! If "by driving" you mean "colonizing,"replied Slipper even though she could see Janis was missing the point.

Like so many women, Slipper felt trying to control a man or a relationship was like trying to pin a Jellyfish to the wall using peanut butter …that's just asking for trouble. Slipper honestly felt the best a girl could expect from a guy was for him to be reasonable. And if he didn't know what that meant he could ask his mother or his father – which meant his mother. Slipper was resigned to just hold on "asbestos she could" (as she liked to say) while life, like a car without shock absorbers rolled down the poorly maintained gravel road of male speed bumps.

"Let me ask you something," asked The Hairy Colonizer, "Have you ever considered hooking up with an alien? I'm only asking after that girl was supposedly kidnapped by an alien and turns out she wasn't kidnapped after all. Somebody shot a video of her kissing and making out with an alien the day before she disappeared. Makes you wonder, doesn't it? I mean, would you hook up with an alien?"

"Have you ever seen an alien? Seriously, they have slimy scaly tails and yellow teeth. I heard they smell like rotten fish. No freaking way I'd even touch one!" said Slipper.

"I'm gonna reserve judgment," said The Hairy Colonizer.

"Well, you can mess around with interspatial relations all you want, but count me out!" said Slipper.

SEVENTEEN

Before meeting Jimmy Disciple on her lawn, Bella rarely missed the Jimmy Disciple Show. She liked to lounge on Bear who typically defaulted into hairy chair mode. Bella would have Laphonso draped across her lap. She'd be feeling relaxed while watching the Pedro of the Enlightened Chihuahua Show. The show could be a little risqué sometimes. But she was a grown woman and liked a little risqué. And, Jeeziz, that dog Pedro! Wasn't he just the cutest thing?

As if in response, Laphonso would wag his tail ever so slightly.

And then it came! The moment when Jimmy Disciple mentioned Bella's name on world-wire TV....

"And a special hello to my new friends out there. I'm talking about Bella and her wonderful children!"

Bella scratched Laphonso's ears and said, "Isn't that Pedro just too much?"

Laphonso yawned.

Bear groaned.

Bella smiled.

EIGHTEEN

Slipper and The Hairy Colonizer returned from walking Laphonso at the same time a drone was hovering by the door delivering their peetzer-pi with toppings of onion, meat/bee-product haste-paste, butterflied snake, anchovies and pik-sy (pickled pig synapse). The pik-sy was for Brain. He was the only one with a stomach for emotional nerve endings.

"Hellmann's! Did we ever mayonnaise that one on the religious dude!" laughed Brain.

"What do you think he wants it for?" Carlo asked while watching the Rev. Al Sharpton interview one of their neighbors, the retired Injustani Colonel, Steven Sing."

"You can call me Colonel Steve," said the Colonel checking his huge watch.

"Hey. I recognize that guy!" shouted Slipper; "I've seen him out walking at night in the neighborhood.

REV. AL SHARPTON – "Colonel Steve Sing, I wanna aks you why these aliens are showing up all over the place ... and why is Mr. Tchump offering this huge reward for someone to catch and bring him one. You have a master's degree in spiritual understanding from The Prestidigitous Trump University of Peshwar, which qualifies you as something of an expert. Just two weeks ago on the Tonight Show with Jimmy Fallon you gave clear and present insight into why Mr. Tchump is buying up orphanages and shutting them down ... shipping the children off to Mexico. You gave us the answer to that one. Now I'm aksing you ... what's Tchump up to with this alien business?"

COLONEL STEVE – "That business with the children was different. In that case Mr. Tchump was a business deal gone wrong because of blowback from his childhood. No ...this buying up national parks is different. I believe he is trying to inflate...or improve his karma."

REV. AL SHARPTON – "And "karma" IS, in fact, what you wrote your senior thesis on, right?"

COLONEL STEVE – "Right-on brother!"

REV. AL SHARPTON –"I am soooo not your brother. Don't start talking like you're a brother! Unnerstanad me?"

COLONEL STEVE – "Sorry."

REV. AL SHARPTON – Okay, so ... applying what you do know, what can we expect from this whole karma chameleon thing?"

COLONEL STEVE – "Well I am not knowing so much about your chameleon, but I will tell you this much; the human karma filter acts like a giant oyster who is every day siphoning and filtering life-mystery things out from the water of experience. Back in my country, The Bahgavita Rimshak likes to say our karma filter is like a tonsil grabbing and extracting the soul of every animal we ever ate along with every squirrel we are running over, every bug we are stepping on. Every being has a soul. And the soul of each and every one of those creatures that we kill... especially those we eat, it must pass through our karma filter to reach liberation and reincarnation in a new life form. That is the karmic law of the universe."

REV. AL SHARPTON – "So... what's the problem here? Does someone like me who hasn't eaten meat or anything other than a few wheat-thins have anything to worry about?"

COLONEL STEVE – "I think you'll be fine. If however, you were to start eating bar-B-Q again clogging up your karma filter not to mention your arteries, and the souls of pigs and chickens were to start piling up, one on top of the other in your filter, it will not turn out so good for you on the day you stand before the God Shiva. Some wise people are saying these clogged karma filters Americans have are what is attracting the aliens to our planet. They say aliens are not coming to do business with us like Mr. Tchump believes. No, they are coming as they do every forty years to harvest an overabundance of souls, which are ripe and ready to harvest. Why do I say this? Well, if you read Ray Bradbury's last book published after his death ..."

REV. AL SHARPTON – "Are you talking about *Ahmed and the Oblivion Machine* or do you mean *Moles Souls And Jelly Rolls*?"

COLONEL STEVE – "*Moles Souls and Jelly Rolls* is the one I'm speaking of ... where in the second chapter you will see Captain Pjnarro speculating that even Salmonella has a Soul. Bradbury goes further in the next chapter creating his corporate leader type ... the man he referred to as Ecco. This Ecco fellow is metaphor for the ecological Anti-Christ ... a capitalist Rumite from Triton who incorporates a super-successful business on Earth by predicting when souls are ready for harvesting."

REV. AL SHARPTON -"So ... Just to summarize ... you're saying these aliens have come to planet Earth because the soul crop is finally ready to harvest."

COLONEL STEVE –"Yes!"

NINETEEN

Later that evening after watching Rev. Al interview Colonel Steven Singh, the Hairy Colonizer and Slipper took Laphonso for his eleven pm walk. Looking up at the night sky they felt uneasy. Was someone ... something watching? Like when the old witch felt Hansel's finger through the cage bars, was someone measuring their harvestability?

"Creepy!" whispered Slipper.

"Lot of creepy shit going down. Like, I meant to ask you if on any of your walks, did you ever bump into that Colonel Steve Sing guy? I think he's the same guy who likes to walk in our neighborhood."

"Yes, I've seen him," whispered Slipper.

"Why are we whispering? Asked The Hairy Colonizer.

"Just... being cautious, I guess. You never know," said Slipper.

"He's sort of a creepy dude – got a fake leg. Did you know that?" asked The Hairy Colonizer.

"I knew there was something I didn't like about him. You know, I really disliked him right off the bat. Something about his smirk," said Slipper.

"Me too...even though I never really talked to him," said The Hairy Colonizer. "I mean, what does it tell you when two people don't like somebody they never even talked to?" asked The Hairy Colonizer.

Before Slipper could answer, The Hairy Colonizer added, "I'll tell you why I don't like him. It's because – and I hate people who racially profile like I'm doing, but I can't help it. I don't like him because he's Injustani!"

Slipper said, "Right. I know from watching The Rev. Al he's an educated well-read military man and we should respect him, but...I don't know. That whole violence thing that Injustani men do to their women ...I don't like it.

"That's a good reason not to like someone, in my book anyway," said The Hairy Colonizer, "You know what else?"

"What?" asked Slipper.

"It makes the hair on the back of my neck stand up when I hear him tapping that fake leg of his with his military whip... or crop...or whatever it is. Whack whack whack. Listen, I know that sounds prejudice, but maybe I am. Maybe I just don't like Injustani men," said Slipper.

"Is it Hinjustani ... or Injumani?" asked The Hairy Colonizer.

"Whatever," said Slipper.

"Still ... where someone's from, that's not a reason not to like them," said The Hairy Colonizer.

"It's only the men I don't like!" said Slipper, "See...I wrote a paper on Injustanistan in high school. I don't know if you are aware of this, but 78% of the time when an Injustani man dies and his wife is still alive, his relatives grab her before she can run away. They wrap her up in the husband's old Sabubbi he was wearing for his circumcision ceremony ...and then they tie her to his dead body and burn her alive on his pyre."

"You're kidding!"

"No."

"That's crazy!"

"It sure is," said Slipper.

"Injustanis are some seriously crazy people," said The Hairy Colonizer looking up at the night sky.

TWENTY

After his TV interview with Rev. Al Sharpton, Colonel Steven Golub-Singh went straight home. He was bone tired. He gave Jimmy and Pedro a quick kiss in the hallway then went straight into the arms of his CareBear© where he collapsed. But before he could sigh and nod off, he noticed Jimmy D. standing in the doorway. As always, Jimmy held Pedro like a squirming ventriloquist dummy moving the dog's mouth to make the dog appear to be asking, "Don't you want to hear what we did today? I mean ... Jimmy and I sometimes wonder why you always have to go straight to your CareBear© and not us. Is it that you don't find us that interesting anymore ... or you don't have time? What is it? Is there a problem? I really hope you are not Facebook-fucking someone online. .. some gross little Injustani boy."

Colonel Steve Golub-Singh controlled himself. He disengaged from his CareBear© and kept his cool by tapping his plastic leg vigorously with his crop. He began doing mouth-shut exercises to empty his mind and control his temper. He consulted the large chronometer he wore on his thin hairy wrist and set the stop watch for fifteen seconds ... enough time according to the guru Rimpal Thumachey Di–El–Kcekktik to calm one's mind-self. He popped a *super pill then* took a deep breath. With his eyes shut tight he mentally grabbed his internal ka spirit by the scruff of its tiny scaly neck and swung the little brain-imp back to center. It had once again been knocked off center at least seven degrees by Jimmy D.'s inane prattle. Calm now, with his ka re-aligned, and barely rolling his eyes, Colonel Steven Golub-Singh quietly asked, "Alright then ... May I ask what have you two been doing today?"

The *super* pill finally kicked in and the Colonel was smiling like a flamingo.

"You tell him, Pedro," Jimmy said to the dog in his arms. This method of having Pedro appear to talk when Jimmy was upset was something he'd learned from their Oral Roberts marriage counselor tape Jimmy bought online. Jimmy had watched all but one of the seven sessions alone even though Colonel Steve had given his word they would watch and listen together. Technically Jimmy had not listened alone. His faithful dog Pedro had been in his arms.

Jimmy calmed his trembling lips as best he could while making it appear the little dog was speaking, "Today ... Jimmy and me took the first step toward catching an alien!"

"Come again?" said Colonel Steve glancing reflexively at his large Chlorodox watch. Eye contact was not advisable when emotionally upset. Was he going to have to swing his ka around again? This was getting to be routine. Really. He re-booted his *super* flamingo smile.

A bit too loud, Jimmy D almost shouted, "I said ... Me and Pedro ... and you, if you want to join us ... we're gonna catch us a freakin alien."

"You don't have to raise your voice. I'm right here. You said you are going to catch the alien?"

"Yes, I said ... "WE are going to catch the alien. WE. Because WE are a family!"

"Okay, fine ... and just how are WE going to catch this alien?" asked Colonel Steve now unable to control the roll of his eyes while winding the big Chlorodox on his wrist again trying to keep his hands busy. His flaming smile was gone, replaced by what his dead sister called his Smee The Crocodile smile.

"Oh, so now you wanna know how," The dog Pedro appeared to say.

"Okay ... I'll be biting. Yes, I want to know how?" said The Colonel shivering with nervous energy. When stressed Colonel Steve's Pakistani accent returned – even after four years of diction and pronunciation classes his mother insisted he take.

"Shall we tell him?" the dog appeared to ask.

"Yes," said Jimmy D giving permission in his own voice. The dog looked relieved.

"Alright, then. Today we took the first step toward catching ourselves an alien," said Jimmy D in his own voice.

"You have been already doing the saying of that," said the Colonel in broken English barely controlling himself.

Jimmy D could not resist correcting his 'friend's' sentence structure ... "I think what you were trying to say was, "You already said that, and yes, Pedro and I took that first step by buying THE ONLY VELOCOPTER ON THE FACE OF THE EARTH!" lip-synced Pedro.

Colonel Steve was dumbfounded and more than a little annoyed. He was a busy man – an important man. According to Colonel Steve, The nation of Injustan (An Islamic protectorate in Northern Waziristan, Pakistan) had once depended on him for security which often meant inflicting horrific pain. It had to be done. A woman named Fatima still phoned from time to time claiming she was from security. That's what she said. But the screaming in the background made hearing difficult and her accent was so thick Jimmy D could hardly understand her. Did anyone know who the Hell anyone really was anymore? Jimmy D now just hung up on her. He gave these people nothing. It was too risky. The Colonel's people were crazy. They were cruel. They were....

Colonel Steve started to say, "Listen, I'm sure what you just said about the velocop machine makes a lot of sense to...someone... " but then Pedro's lip-synced words began to sink in. The *super* pill began producing a secondary high. A cheap high from pills was one of America's perks. Was it the pills that made the Colonel interested now? Although two new messages had arrived via alert-buzz on his wrist-chlonoglyph, Colonel Steve did not answer them. He shut off his phone. He stuck it in a drawer. He'd heard the new watch technology enabled hackers to watch you when the phone was turned off. The Colonel Steve's wrist-chlonoglyph was a repurposed early wind-up model hand-made by the best jeweler in Indurostan City in the early part of the 20th century. During renovation anything could have been installed. You just never knew. Colonel Steve Golub-Singh had insisted on maintaining the spring wind mechanism when he'd had it modernized with updates that included apps for receiving electro-message teloportol and 70mkg Gubordoflight. Again, who knows what other spy and reverse spy programs they installed. He did insist on a solar ionization over-ride in case he forgot to wind it. But that was rarely necessary as Colonel Steve was man of meticulous habit and fastidious planning which kept him balanced and grounded like a 10foot copper shaft buried in bedrock. Winding his watch was part of his daily ritual.

"Go on … I'm listening," said Colonel Steve Golub-Singh wishing to God he didn't have to go through this role playing charade every time Jimmy wanted to tell him something. He was so sick of the stupid dog-man pantomime. The Chinese had the right idea. They ate Goddamned dogs!

"Okay … Here's how it went down … " Jimmy D said through ventriloquy with Pedro appearing to describe the transaction with the kids and Bella ending with Jimmy having to leave the velocopter at Carlo's house.

"Well, I have the answer," said Colonel Steve Golub-Singh who now remembered seeing pictures of velocopters during his military training.

"And doesn't Colonel Know-it-all always have the answer!" snarked Pedro.

"I didn't graduate top of my class at Punjabi War College for being a dummy!" laughed Colonel Steve Golub-Singh.

"Well, what is your brilliant idea?" asked Pedro.

"We use my uncle's school bus to pick it up," said Colonel Steve Golub-Singh.

"That piece of crap?" asked Jimmy D. not even bothering to use his ventriloquist voice, "When was the last time you had that thing running?"

"You got a better idea … let's hear it?" said Colonel Steve Golub-Singh getting a little annoyed, "A little tinkering and tuning to get the engine running and we'll go pick the thing up." said Colonel Steve, "End of story!"

"Seriously? That piece of crap hasn't run since you and your buddies went hunting up in Alabama and had to limp home in … what was it, second gear?"

"Like I said, if you have a better idea ...I'm all ears!" said Colonel Steve now wearing his infamous rana-fusca Henry Kissinger smile ... that same frog-like grin he'd flashed years ago toward Jimmy D at The Gay Bar of Jesus Disciples ... the smile which first caught Jimmy D's eye.

"C'mon... let's go take a look!" said Colonel Steve Golub-Singh tapping his plastic leg and hitching it around careful not to step on the little dog, Pedro.

TWENTY-ONE

The following evening after dinner Slipper and Carlo took Laphonso for his walk. As they strolled around the block Carlo said, "Can I ask you something, Slipper?"

They had that kind of relationship where they felt free to bounce ideas off each other ... almost brother and sister. Carlo sometimes wondered, if his father was still alive would he have been comfortable asking the old man personal questions ... things about sex and girls. Although Carlo loved and respected his mother, they did not have that kind of relationship. Carlo and Brain never talked about girls. Grampa Joe? You gotta be kidding. Sometimes Carlo buried his face in Laphonso's neck fur and confided in the dog. But that was limited by Laphonso's inability to speak English ... a one-way street. At the same time, Carlo was pretty sure humans and dogs got along as well as they did precisely because dogs don't talk. Communing by burying your nose in a dog's fur had the added benefit of the dog's wonderful leafy woodsy smell.

"Yeah, sure," answered Slipper.

"No biggie ... only ... well ... oh it's nothing," said Carlo.

"C'mon ... you can't go askin' permission to ask ... getting' me all interested and then chicken out," said Slipper giving Carlo a soft punch on the arm.

"Okay," said Carlo, "I mean ... it's just that every time I think about girls ... women ... I kinda have to go through the whole process of explaining to myself how you girls are different from us men," said Carlo.

"Like how?" asked Slipper.

"Well, like ... with me ... I have to re-assure myself that women actually like us men ...me in particular ...and that you actually like sex. I mean, in the back of my mind I think you might just love babies... and that you know you need us to have babies so you put up with us. I think these things every time I think about approaching a girl," he said.

"Believe me ... we like sex," she said, "And some of us don't give a rat's ass about babies. And, I guess there are those who just want you for making babies. "

Carlo continued, "Well, like, I mean ... you have a pussy ... a vagina and all. You don't have a penis or balls. And you have boobs. I still don't get the whole breast thing ... you know, like, when does it feel good for you to get touched there and when doesn't it? And, what's with the nipples? Are they sensitive like little penises or are they like my nipples, which don't really do a whole lot unless some jerk pinches them ... and that hurts. But you girls make such a big deal over your tits. Sometimes you act like you want em played with. Most times, though, it's like you'll scratch our eyes out if we so much as look at em cross-eyed ... even though you got em hanging out exposed practically down to your belly button. Does any of this make sense?" asked Carlo.

Slipper replied, "Well, the only thing I can tell you is that there's no one explanation fits all girls. We've all had different experiences. Some girl maybe had a bad brother who pinched her tits for years making her hate the idea of a boy touching her there. I know this girl who had a bad uncle who would cop a feel if he could get her alone in the garage. So she was surprised when she started going out with this guy who really didn't find her tits all that interesting after he saw them and felt them once or twice. I mean, you guys all different too, right? I mean, except that you're all totally ruled by your penises like us."

"Yeah, I suppose," said Carlo.

"Guys really are inept in that sense. I mean, God, a girl can literally lead guys around by their cocks. You're kind of pathetic!"

"Yeah, I suppose," said Carlo.

TWENTY-TWO

All her life, The Hairy Colonizer wanted to become a revered biologist. She was always stymied by a lack of funds for school. But she'd done work-study and gotten scholarships and was only a semester away from her master's degree. She had student loan debt up the wazoo, but so what! She had a sense of self worth that was priceless. In high school she read books by known biologists the way other kids read teen romance novels. Her favorite of the LaCandy Slutporn Smith-Martin, Girl Detective Series was titled "Gory Bacteria Girl." This featured the pimply adolescent, Pamela, who solved crimes in an impromptu lab she set up by herself in her bedroom on the make-up table her Super Model mother gave her for Christmas. Using basic bacteria analysis there was no crime Bacteria Girl could not solve. She grew colonies of incriminating bacteria lifted from such unlikely places as undershorts and cat litter boxes. In her last book titled *Gory Bacteria Girl*, Pamela swiped a sample of hedge fund CEO Thomas Hareston's bacteria from his bicycle seat after one of his bouts with irritable bowel syndrome. This turned out to be a game changer. Who knew Mr. Moneybags liked to ride around the Hamptons nude after midnight?

The Hairy Colonizer obsessed on bacteria while growing up. Where the tiny swarming microbes grossed out other kids, she couldn't get enough.

"Slipper ... do you ever think about how life got here billions of years ago?" asked The Hairy Colonizer while they were walking Laphonso, "I mean ... I believe something or someone must have come here from outer space. They didn't just grow here on this planet spontaneously. These bacteria saw an opportunity to colonize a planet and they pounced on it! Bam! They're a perfect fit for an empty planet like Earth. They're perfect. They can manipulate their own DNA. That's the key. I mean, like, how much different was that than us humans figuring out how to harness the pig or the horse? No big deal, right? I mean, us forcing horses carry us around ... carry our mail ... plow our fields? I mean, not just the horse, but the dog, the elephant. There are so many creatures WE trained to do our bidding. Jeziz, we even got plants doing what we tell them now. I mean, who'd a thought ten years ago we'd be getting electricity from trees? Certainly not Republicans, of course. So, why is it so hard to get on board with the idea of bacteria based electrics? And harnessing DNA to build some sort of living vehicle they could drive around in and on when they first arrived on this hostile Earth is a no-brainer. Come on! It's soooooo obvious. Hello! They built us! Not God! Bacteria made us. Halejulia, praise Bacteria! Get down on your knees and praise bacteria almighty! They built the early humanoids using DNA architecture. Did they design us to be life-vehicles to gather up food and nutrients for them? You bet they did! And over time ... and we're talking about billions of years here, our simple bacteria-built robot ancestors kept improving and through mutation eventually morphing billions of years later into ... ta da! ... you and me! I'm talking a bacterial-evolution revolution!"

Slipper pondered before responded with a question, "You really believe we're just bacteria built horse carts that got out of control? And ... then those carts turned into us human beings ... and we went on to build cities and cars and shopping centers?" asked Slipper.

"Why is that so hard to believe?" asked The Hairy Colonizer.

"You have to ask?" asked Slipper.

"Look," said The Hairy Colonizer , "Something or someone had to build the first humans. Why not bacteria? And I reject the "God Built US theory" because bacteria make a Hell of a lot more sense? Jeeziz, I mean, trying to believe that God took the trouble to build us ... just so he could punish us for having sex ... and so we could worship him ... that's sooooooo lame!"

"Well, I admit it is kinda lame," said Slipper.

"Take my word for it. It was bacteria!" said The Hairy Colonizer, "Do you have any idea how many different types of bacteria are living inside you at any given time?" asked The Hairy Colonizer.

"Five? Fifty? Okay, I give up," answered Slipper,

"Over 100,000." said The Hairy Colonizer with her eyes flashing and an aura of bacteria circling her head like a halo.

"You know, when you get excited like that, you're really quite beautiful," said Slipper.

"Thank you. You're not bad yourself ... for a control freak."

TWENTY-THREE

The Hairy Colonizer was not sure how she felt about Laphonso sucking rabbit ears. The rabbits came out of his mouth wet with dog saliva ... like movie stars with their fur all slicked down ... like Elvis. But wasn't a dog supposed to chase rabbits, not suck them? Watching Laphonso and the rabbits play, The Hairy Colonizer asked Slipper, "Did you ever wonder something for years and not understand it ... then all of a sudden hear bells going off in your head?"

"You know, I'm still pretty much wondering about everything," replied Slipper.

"I'm talking about that "aha moment" ... you know, when something suddenly becomes clear." said The Hairy Colonizer.

"Can't say I have," replied Slipper.

"See, here's the thing ... ever since I was a little girl and first saw black hairs growing down around my possum I've wondered why us girls have pubic hair ... not that I mind it."

"Well, yeah, some men think it's kind of ugly." answered Slipper.

"Exactly!" said The Hairy Colonizer, "Why do we have ugly man-hair growing all up and down our legs and on our ass? Bella says that a lot of girls stopped shaving in the sixties. But it grossed the guys out so they started shaving again. See... I like keeping the guys at bay ... sort of a test. If they're not man enough to deal with a woman's natural body hair ... they won't pass go!" said The Hairy Colonizer.

"I don't know. You ask me, the whole arrangement down there would be so much nicer without the hair. Flowers aren't all hairy. Why should we be hairy?" asked Slipper.

"For the longest time I thought that too. Couldn't figure out why anyone would inflict that ugly hair on us. And quite frankly, when I first looked at my bush in this little hand mirror my mother gave me, honest to God, Slipper, I almost fainted. It looked like a bearded dragon. I thought there was something wrong with me."

"I know what you mean," said Slipper, "I was scared that the first guy who got a look at me down there would run out of the room."

"Me too," laughed The Hairy Colonizer.

"Don't get me wrong. It does scare a few. Turns some of em gay I heard. But with most guys, honestly we could have a dead skunk down there and they wouldn't even notice they're so over-the-top bonkers at getting something, anything inside a vagina."

"Okay ... but see, I was on to something when I was asking why anyone would inflict all that ugly hair on us. Because that "anyone" is the key! Who was that "anyone" who would do that? Bingo! It was Mr. Bacteria, that's who!"

"Sometimes you scare me," said Slipper.

"No...come on, just listen. Mr. Bacteria, not God, is responsible for us ladies having a big thatch of pubic hair!" said The Hairy Colinizer.

"Explain please," said Slipper.

"It came to me like a slap in the face after I read this article on the internet talking about how much healthier vaginally delivered babies are than babies delivered cesarean ... at least in terms of allergies. Turns out doctors are convinced that vagina delivered babies get a slime coat of their mothers' bacteria while sliding out through the mother's thatch of public hair. TA DA ... ALL THE BEST BACTERIA IS HANGING OUT RIGHT THERE AT THE OPENING GROWING ON THE PUBIC HAIR ... JUST WAITING TO JUMP ONTO THAT BABY!"

"Hey! Look up there!" cried Slipper, "A shooting star!"

"Could be another incoming hot blob of bacteria. "

"Do you suppose?"

"It wouldn't surprise me."

BLUE MOON
PART II

For part 2 we travel back to December 23 1945 for our first encounter with Albert Einstein. Sorry for any inconvenience this mental time shift may cause.

TWENTY-FOUR

EARTH – Dec. 21, 1945.

Storefronts in New Orleans declared: "Only four more shopping days till Christmas!" Front page of the Times Picayune mourned General Patton's death. Everyone was looking forward to Christmas. Trying to follow an Earth calendar was confusing for the Eins ... like learning a new language. There were quite a few Eins here on Earth from the planet Torrik. Unless you knew what to look for you couldn't tell them from Earthlings. Though generally good natured, some of their intentions were less than honorable, especially those here on business.

No one suspected that the two hooded figures strolling past the bright Christmas window displays were not Christmas shoppers, but were, in fact, Eins. These two were typically short with heavily bearded faces and long frizzy hair. They wore shapeless moleskin greatcoats. Holiday light glinted off the larger one's ironized glasses. Their red beards glowed like electrified copper scouring pads.

"Just keep your wits about you!" said the larger one known simply as The Commissioner. He had an exceptionally long nose housing a deep resonating chamber, which reverberated his every articulation. His vocal cords were frayed from barking commands all his life. And from his rumbling gravely masculine speech, anyone from Torikk would know immediately something had gone wrong with his "operation."

125

TWENTY-FIVE

The Operation

After nearly twenty years of devastating wars, Dame Lola was fed up. She and 99% of her fellow women on Torikk were disgusted with the clot of savage impotent old men arranging wars for their sons to fight. As leader of the Council of Women, Dame Lola announced she would organize a Galaxy-wide symposium at the Edgecomb Diad where she would present her case.

At the Edgecomb Diad Lola passed around a binder listing page after page of male transgressions across the Galaxy. She waved her binder in the air while she lambasted male selfishness. The old generals snidely referred to her findings as "The Gonad Report" because it blamed male hormones for practically all problems. To be fair, the report did document scientific studies showing males were generally unwilling and unable to control their emotions and behavior leading to galaxy-wide suffering. The report concluded beyond reasonable doubt that male aggression had been the cause of 94% of all misunderstandings, slaughters, and retribution killings since record keeping began over a thousand psi-florinad.

At the Edgecomb Diad, Dame Lola and over 140 million female Torikks signed and sealed with their menstrual blood an edict demanding from that day forward, all male children borne from their womanly wombs would have their psycho-deviator complexes and their guriads removed at birth.

Highly controversial, this might not have become the law of the land and the Galaxy had not one man, The Commissioner, Torikk's most decorated war hero, thrown his support behind it. After The Commissioner came out in favor he had to evade a phalanx of assassins there to stop him as he stood shoulder to shoulder with Dame Lola at The Edgcomb Diad. But stand with her in that glorious moment, he did!

In every society there are iconic moments. Today there is not a man or woman on Torikk who does not remember the night when the one called simply The Commissioner, standing beside Lola before the entire House of Lords, delivered a fiery demand for passage ending with this famous quote...

"... and let this, the will of our women come to pass! Too long has the Galaxy suffered under the tyranny of unregulated testosterone! I say, I DEMAND ... LET THIS BILL PASS!"

After his speech he was smiling and pointing "hellos" to the assembled dignitaries when Colonel Shandusky Einfarb of Tallibaggio emerged from an electro-visual fog. Later it was learned Shandusky was pumped up with a nearly lethal dose of hydro-testosterone. He staggered toward The Commissioner's back. The entire planet watched in horror. Some screamed warnings but to no avail as Shandusky swung his white-hot cutto again and again hacking and hewing at the Commissioner's shoulder until The Commissioner's left arm dangled from a single sinew. Rose-colored blood spurted onto a dozen camera lenses. The last cutto blow glanced off the shoulder and caught The Commissioner's jaw laying him out on the stage motionless for all the world to see. Things looked bad for Lola and her brave female followers. Alas it seemed their hard fought victory would be stolen by a single act of the very violence they were hoping to erase, violence by agents of Torikk's bloated male-dominated defense industry.

Torikk history throbs with stories of frontier justice. Scooping the Commissioner's twitching severed arm from the floor and clutching it by its wrist like some bloody cudgel, Lola advanced on Shandusky as he paraded drunkenly about the stage with his arms raised in victory. Swinging the bloody arm like a club Lola delivered a blow to the side of Shandusky's large bearded head ... caught him flat against the temple. Shandusky fell on top of The Commissioner. Though trapped under the general's weight, The Commissioner managed to unscabber his own cutto and with barely enough time for the ceramic edge to reach a dull red glow, The Commissioner decapitated Shandusky with one swipe. The horrifying hiss and gurgle of hot sword edge cutting soft fatty double-chin flesh was caught live for the ages on electro-vision. To this day a permanent call-up flip-view is available for everyone to see on eye-daddy.

But The Commissioner was not done. With blood still pulsing from his mangled shoulder, and supported on his side by a blood-soaked Lola, he staggered forward and grabbed the magnificent central hall silver ear. With his voice amplified a hundred times he shouted, "My friends. I am badly wounded. But I would gladly suffer ten times the suffering of such wounds if it means peace is at last coming to our beloved planet. I go now to the hospital... and while there I will volunteer to undergo the first psycho-deviator complex removal."

He collapsed in Lola's arms.

Here's where stories differ. Some say there were complications in the operating room. One old troublemaker General named Edguardo The Evincer blamed the female doctors who insisted on performing the operation, for its failure. Edguardo claimed the woman doctors had educations inferior to their male counterparts. Whatever the reason, while attempting to re-attach The Commissioner's severed arm and on the same day remove his male complex, both operations failed. The Commissioner did not die, but he was never the same. He was maimed.

Afterward, The Commissioners' enemies attempted to portray him as a buffoon. In war rooms, thick with cigar smoke and saddle soap, old colonels and generals sniggered as they repeated the prevailing joke about The Commissioner's arm and maleo-guriad complexor getting switched in the operating room resulting in his guriad getting sewn, stapled and glued back on to his shoulder. This misplaced organ, they joked, hung uselessly most of the time but would bulge obscenely whenever a young woman approach his left side. They would tell this joke and laugh until they cried. They never tired of this joke.

The Commissioner's operation was not the only one to get botched. At least twenty of the early operations encountered problems. Those who volunteered were awarded the Medal of Honor. Today the procedure is second nature and nearly 100% safe...simple as a circumcision.

The Commissioner was awarded The Medal of Honor. And, of course, all his teeth were removed and replaced with gold!

TWENTY-SIX

1945

"You know, I really hope he doesn't behave like the tsteffisole they say he is," The Commissioner muttered. Then he reconsidered, "But then again ... maybe It would be better if he did."

Struggling with his equipment, Abel snorted agreement. Double-barbed needles on four-foot lightweight pikes nearly as tall as Abel jabbed inside his greatcoat. Beads of sweat trickled down his back short-circuiting diodes and frog-switches. Even though The Commissioner could hear the electric arc-snaps and he could see Abel's eyes open wide with each shock, he made mental note that Abel was a real soldier. He never complained. Probably because Abel, like The Commissioner, still had one testosterone-producing guriad.

They continued up S. Clairborne Avenue passing through the Tulane University gate. They walked past a hand-lettered sign on a wrought iron stand outside Dixon Hall announcing – ALBERT EINSTEIN LECTURE ON TIME MECHANICS TODAY AT 4:30 room 110.

The lecture had already begun by the time they entered. Albert Einstein was standing stiff and formal at his lectern wearing a wool herringbone jacket and wrinkled wool pants. The Commissioner was good at summing them up at a glance. This Einstein fellow looked arrogant.

Abel considered this assignment just another day's work. Better than sitting behind a desk. The Commissioner, however, was annoyed at the assignment. He had not worked his ass off to become some interplanetary disciplinarian ... had not sacrificed an arm and his social life to become an enforcer! But rules were rules, weren't they? And unless you sent an Aarbot, with the good sense of a toaster, what or who would you send?

Trying to draw as little attention as possible they took seats in the back, seats from which they could leave in a hurry. But having been on ice for at least forty pounds (Time in Torikk is measured in pounds per square unit) of pressurized carbon tetra-dioxide they did not feel exactly limber, The Commissioner and Able rustled and twitched in their seats! This annoyed the steel haired lady sitting in front of them who turned around to frown at them. Looking straight into The Commissioner's eyes, she shushed him each time he rustled. But The Commissioner was a man of discipline and paid no attention.

TWENTY-SEVEN

Albert Einstein glanced at his tattered notebook from time to time as he spoke. He had a noticeable German accent and his audience hung on his every word ... "There's been a tendency on our part to look at this thing vee call time like it was just some *tic toc, tic toc* from clock, right? But, some of you are going to have to change the vvay you look "time" because time is more than a tangle of nano-seconds and minutes spewing out behind our clocks like some wake from a speedboat! Much more! Here, let me show you. Where the Hell is za chalk? Ah! Okay."

As Einstein wrote on the chalkboard behind him, the crowd began to murmur.

"... so vee see here (tapping his chalk on the board annoyingly) time is a direct function of enerchy ... and ven vee factor in the moment of coincidence over a vector slant ... what I like to call entropy, and then cook the whole business over a constant millennium factor, it becomes apparent to anyone vits half a brain that ... TIME ... HAS ... MASS! My God, you can weight it!"

He looked out on his audience smiling, waiting for what he'd just said to sink in. Then he turned back to the board and continued, "Okay, so now we have time with her mass moving in a constant direction toward an infinity line ... (writing furiously now) ... and if we follow that line a little further ... we see that we get ... (writing even faster and ending with a flourish) ENERGY!!! Do you see that? We get time converting herself to ... ENERGY!!!"

The commissioner looked around nervously when the steel haired lady stood up as if she were at a concert and cheered. A few followed her example. But most people in the room grumbled.

Some started to boo.

Then a fight broke out between an older gentleman who must have been in his eighties and a nerdy looking young man wearing a white lab coat – a graduate student? People tried to separate them, but they kept going back at each other until security arrived in black leather jackets and shiny black shoes to drag the two of them from the room.

When the crowd got quiet Einstein began speaking again.

"I had no idea physics inspired so much passion," he said. The crowd laughed nervously.

"But, anyway, if my theory is correct, Einstein continued, "... and I think it is, because as you know, I'm pretty good at the math. (more laughter from the crowd) "If I am right, then something odd is happening ... or better I should say, is going to happen. In the year 2025, this phenomenon I have just identified as time in my equations, she will do something we have never seen her do before. And because time will act so unpredictable ... I call her a she."

Here he faced the audience with a hollow ... almost puzzled expression – as if even he couldn't believe what he was saying.

"Time ...she WILL convert herself into a protean belt of plasmic vibrating light! And then, if her energy is not absorbed or somehow bled off, she will begin to concentrate into herself. What was once time will turn into energy, a combination of heavy mass basic elements of energy. Slowly at first and then with increasing speed, doubling at each time-energy-mass event, she will increase her mass until she becomes so heavy that her gravity begins to exceed that of the earth. Then this black hole of time will begin tugging at everything we know and love, first at the clouds, then at the rain and the sea and the oceans ... and then before vee can even scream, the mountains and the earth's very core will be torn inside out and together with all memory ... all life ... everything ... will be pulled into a bottomless gravitational pit to vanish forever!

Some in the crowd must have had an inkling of what the crazy professor was going to say, for they pulled unpleasant objects from their pockets, book bags and backpacks and threw them at the old coot up on stage. On the other hand, there were the defenders of Einstein who fought back at these naysayers. Noses got punched and bloodied, lips got split. It wasn't the violence, however, that got to Einstein, it was the laughter.

As we know from Palmer's work with mules, nothing gets the goat of a man aspiring to Godliness angrier than laughter. Raging inside, his face, tomato sauce red, Albert Einstein stomped his foot.

"SILENCE!" he shouted.

And for a moment his command seemed to have cowed the crowd under his control again. But then somebody threw a sausage-shaped piece of dog excrement, which blindsided the old scientist and lodged in his hair. He tried to remove it, but only succeeded in smearing it into his long frizzy hair. Laughter swelled like two ocean swells peaking, tossing the scientist into a paroxysm of rage. He stormed off the stage, his papers flying behind him like a comet's tail. His glasses fell and he accidentally stepped on them breaking both lenses. Somehow he found and buttoned his coat one button off alignment as he muttered his way out the rear fire exit.

TWENTY-EIGHT

Two figures waited for Einstein outside the back door. Abel had primed and loaded two carbon tipped harpoons taken from under his coat. The moment Einstein emerged, The Commissioner spun him around with his one strong arm and pinned him to the ground kneeling astride his thin chest. Abel jabbed prongs from the sleek harpoons into Einstein's shoulder and neck. Small blue sparks flew. Einstein's eyes bulged then he went limp...then almost immediately snapped rigid. The Commissioner felt a slight electric contact tingle.

With Einstein incapacitated, Abel withdrew the probes, folded them, then put them back under his coat. While The Commissioner attached the virtual albatross around Einstein's neck, Abel snap-clasped what looked like two suitcase handles to Einstein's rigid back. Side by side they carried him to their ship. Next stop Torikk where Einstein would stand trial for giving humans the atomic bomb. If found innocent, the virtual albatross would be removed. If found guilty he would wear it for the rest of his life.

TWENTY-NINE

Who are These Eins?

On Planet Torikk in the heart of Galaxy K-14, the concept of time is measured differently than on Earth. Some say that's why their lives can span up to two centuries. An inner metabolic proto-platform slows their heart rates to near zero when they sleep. On another level, they measure time's passage, NOT with a clock or a calendar, but with a DP *differential pressure gauge*, which measures time as a function of energy. These DP carbolic dioxidal gauges are living entities which are harvested from living plants. Like pets, these timepieces are treated like family members. Problems, of course, arise if and when DP timepieces feel slighted, real or perceived. A Torikk comedian can count on an easy laugh with a joke about his clock. He can also get a laugh joking about the infamous Ein absent-mindedness. But there are two things a comedian cannot joke about, one is the young male's "operation" and the other is the massive energy burst in store for planet 890kl (Earth) which many still believe is a result of Torikk meddling.

Nearly all males and females on Torikk get personally involved in the sciences. Everyone's a scientist and everyone has a different opinion...on everything. And that's good. On each subject, Jet propulsion, electrical engineering, genetics, every individual gets personally invested. Some say it's because Torikk women took over...others disagree. But there's one thing EVERY Torikk agrees on; in (the year) fifty-four pounds per square (Earth year 2025) a massive energy burst is in store for planet 890kl (Earth) which is considered by many on Torikk as an intellectually stagnant backwater. Making jokes about Earthlings would be like making jokes about retarded people or when someone falls in the Special Olympics. Earth is where conservative Neanderthal politicians dance the ego-bump cha-cha – the planet where climate-change deniers hired by Earth's oil and coal industries buy off the honor of anyone in a position of responsibility – the place where an ignorant populace believes practically every political lie. Is it a wonder Earth was a Mecca for scam artists from all across the galaxy?

Unfortunately, as Einstein said in his lecture, in fifty-four pounds per square (the year 2025) planet Earth has a cosmic date with destiny. Earth is scheduled to first implode then explode from inner forces of a planetary time-fueled energy burst.

Earth's will not be the first energy burst to occur in Galaxy K14. Nearly sixty-eight PSI ago planet 566ab78 imploded. And though that was bad news for her inhabitants (nearly every inhabitant was incinerated) there was the collateral benefit of easily convertible iron-core energy which splattered out hundreds of foiltomes into space where it could be easily harvested without permit or license.

Torikks, when referring to a planet undergoing a millennium burst, will use the pronoun "her" to further the "milking" metaphor. Millennium bursts produce gobs of thick white milky iron hydride amalgam … 99% pure energy flying out into space. During planet 566ab78's energy burst nearly every able-bodied ship in the galaxy made the trip to anchor-bounce in what was left of a gravity orbit while sucking up as much fuel as they could store. In most cases they harvested mega-metric tons per square for merely the cost of making the trip.

Much progress had been made since 566ab78's implosion in the field of Planet dynamics. In fact, today it would be easy to milk off the iron bi-hydrocaustic event in store for Earth and save its inhabitants were it not for the interstellar economic shutdown which caused a ten-fold INCREASE in the price of space travel, not to mention the fact that Earth's rotation belt is near the outer edge of the Galaxy – a prohibitively long way off! And, of course, it would be an even longer trip back because Earth is on the opposite side of the magna belt meaning a heavily laden cargo ship would have to beat its way back against the cosmic tide!

But more than anything, there are the new laws. Unlike back when planet 566ab78 had gushed its energy milk, such fueling expeditions are highly regulated today. Non-interference laws were enacted following serious abuse by the biggest international Ein Scopees and their agents. These newly passed "intello-factor laws" as they are called, regulate the manner in which intelligent life can legally interface with not-so-intelligent life. These laws allow little or no contact between species and to insure this, over five hundred planets were given the designation of nature preserves. These laws alone would give pause to anyone considering an expedition to Earth. Recently Torikks were allowed access to previously classified Ein Documents and video. Films by Albert Einstein's own clone-meister showed the havoc wreaked by Scopees posing as humans ... walking, dressing and talking like them in order to take advantage of low Earth intelligence.

Albert Einstein and his Ein Torikk Scopee agents were unable to resist when greedy human leaders approached Scopee agents metaphorically slithering on their bellies offering to sell out the futures of their own grandchildren for the Torikk equivalent of beads and baubles. The most popular items humans sought as bribes were firearms of any type and, of course, anti-gravity velocopters (all now returned and accounted for except one). And of course, everyone wanted the atomic bomb.In the final days Torikk news sources plastered images of returning archeological Scopee scientists in frozen-state aboard Tru-master ships. Each Scopee had the virtual Albatross hung around his neck fastened by Galaxy police ... reminiscent of Samuel Taylor Coleridge's poem, The Rime Of The Ancient Mariner, which was, in fact, plagiarized from an ancient Torikk fable of good and evil. Coleridge apparently slipped a copy under his waistcoat while in the recovery room aboard a science research space frigate which was visiting Earth in the 18th century. Apparently Torikk nurses forgot he was still aboard. With the stolen polamard script fable hidden in his waistband, Coleridge lowered himself from the ship using bed sheets and went home to transcribe the story into poetry in 1797. The rest is history.

THIRTY

Nearly two hundred twenty nine earth years later...defying laws and logic, one lone space frigate, The Beagle HU-X2 steams toward planet Earth. At the controls floating upon a hover-cushion of carbon gas sits an elderly Ein wearing the shameful albatross around his neck. His frizzy hair is unkempt from his habit of running worried trembling fingers through it while monitoring a bio-plasma screen. FYI, the biomeme of each and every Ein originate from one basic gene sequence created by ancient bacteria on Planet Torikk long before recorded history. This accounts for the similarity of all Eins' appearance. The name, Albert Einstein, is embroidered in bar code gold thread on the pocket of his dark blue yellow star-spotted uniform.

He is been out on parole from frozen gas prison only a few decades. But he will always wear the virtual albatross around his neck. Torikk justice is fair, harsh, and as Ein history will tell you, marbled like a Kobii rollo steak with humor. All on Torikk agree humor is what distinguishes intelligent species from their lesser I.Q. cousins in the Galaxy. Torikks take great pleasure in citing lower I.Q. Earth creatures who try to make up for their poor understanding of humor by including LOL in their posts alerting readers when to laugh.

Strangely beautiful geometric icons dance in green hallo-graph thruster-glide across Albert's holoid screen filling out a jigger-stylized ikat scroll. These patterns Albert compares to vegetable dyed weavings which fascinated him so many years ago on Planet Earth before The Commissioner came for him.

"Bastard!" he mutters at the constant reminder of the normally weightless virtual albatross around his neck. Only when his thoughts stray into illegal territory does the albatross gain noticeable weight. If his bad thinking continues the virtual sea bird will begin a keening wail.

As a young Torikk living on Earth, Albert enjoyed hiking high into The Red Horn Valley of the Hindu Kush. On such trips he collected antique weavings which graced the tents of nomadic high-desert people. He'd loved Gurgeiff's antique Oriental rug collection. Up in the mountains beyond international boundaries Albert was intrigued that many of modern Earth life's changes were still vague as fog bone. He'd laughed and smoked hashish with the villagers. He'd eaten garlic mutton skewered on willow sticks. These villagers were steeped in tradition thick and sharp as cheddar aged in goatskin. And he'd fallen in love with a young mountain girl. But it was not to be.

His computer-generated ica-forms remind Albert of those bi-gone days. Primitive as the Earthlings were, they possessed the power to love. Something Eins and Scopees were capable of, but to a much lesser degree. One was never moon-struck with love on Torikk. There are no love poems.

There had been undeniable similarities between Kush dancers and Torikk modern dance, of which Albert is a great fan and supporter. Torikk dance still colors its steps outside the lines of traditional morals. Normally law-abiding citizens on Torikk would cue-up outside unlicensed Alborin houses hoping to purchase a ten-minute virtual sexual encounter with a naked outlaw l.e.x.d. Dancer. Some say this is the result of shadow art donated by otherwise shadow-grown souls? Oh, the horror! Oh the delight!

"Doogooders," Albert cackles at the thought of pinko morality checkers. He grins as he watches the dancers despite the growing weight and electric prick of his albatross. He allows himself to be mesmerized by memories of those brief days when he experienced Earthly love. His eyes are nearly closed and his head rocks from side to side when a message pops hot red upon the screen...

ENERGY LEVEL CRITICAL

ENERGY LEVEL CRITICAL

BLUE ALERT PLEASE.

BLUE ALERT

THIRTY-ONE

Across the ship alarms scream.

BLUE ALERT! ENERGY LEVEL CRITICLY LOW.

BLUE ALERT! ENERGY LEVEL CRITICLY LOW

An odd thumping shakes the ship. Sparks flash from loose and, according to Pilot, shoddy circuitry ... EARTH ORBIT ACHIEVED. BLUE ALERT! ENERGY LEVEL CRITICALLY LOW

"Okay! Okay!" The Ein floating beside Albert hisses, "We know we need energy. Why the foo-fotch do you think we're here?"

This Ein's name is Pilot. He collects himself and mumbles calmly into his helmet, "We won't use excess energy if we just orbit here for a while... kill some time until we can refuel off the carcass."

Because they all look alike, Earthlings often mistake Eins for twins or at least siblings. These Eins aboard the ship are named Ein-Pilot, Ein-Terrier, and Dahlia (Her ghoto-card official name is Dali-Ein). Also aboard the ship is one flash-frozen passenger whose lanyard identifies him only as Roberto Rothsbanyo.

Pilot complains, "Fotch it to Goshen! I knew it was a bad idea to sail out here in this old crate. The bastard Sharpstein knew full well she burns fuel like some starving blowbelly! (Pilot mimics Sharpstein who sold them the ship and is not aboard) ... *Uh ... No problem, General (he* calls everyone general) ... *you'll be going out with the cosmic tide. It's just a small diversion for you to approach Earth."*

This after they informed Sharpstein the ship needed fuel and would have to alter course to obtain it from Earth.

"No problem. Hey, after you pick up the fuel cream you can pitch-pole your way back if you want. I mean, you're gonna have enough extra energy to cook an albatross. Ha Ha Ha. "

Sharpstein's albatross reference elicits half a snigger from Pilot at Albert's expense. Allbert tugs at his albatross and gives Pilot the stink-eye.

Pilot says, "Fotch it, man, it wasn't me who gave Earthlings the theory of relativity. I mean, everyone except you knew they couldn't handle it."

Now, after weeks in space tempers were raw. It had become abundantly clear just how beat-up, bent, and poorly equipped The Beagle HUX2 really was and worse yet, how fast she was burning through fuel. It didn't help that Terrier forgot to change co-ordinates after they'd passed through The Lesser Starfield Grandway, forcing them to drift nearly three beams off their original route. It wasn't until they were in the clear harsh light of space they got their first shocking glimpse of The Beagle HUX2's outer structure. They could see, outlined like a skeleton, where the Beagle's outer membrane had been pushed in by a million gamma brads pelting against her over the years. The outer film-skin was as soft as titanium foil in some places. Sharpstein had apparently hid this from them beneath a hastily applied scale coat which began flaking off and drifting away after the first 20 pounds of pressure folinoid (about a week)

Again Pilot imitates Sharpstein's grating whine, *"Ya got my personal guarantee!"*

Pilot mumbles to himself in a low voice, "Fotchin lot of good some nitro-foot's promise going to do you when we're depressurizing at 40K a second."

And again the alarms and the message...

BLUE ALERT

ENERGY LEVEL CRITICLY LOW

ENERGY LEVEL CRITICLY LOW.

PREPARE TO FOLLOW EMERGENCY EARTH LANDING PROCEDURE.

THIRTY-TWO

All clocks aboard the Beagle HU-X2 go into a full spasm. Their fifteen hands spin wildly. Their dials, gauges, metrical indicators, faces and bodies start bloating then contracting inside their individual conspastic gas drop-down emergency squeeze bags.

Alarms blare out annoying high-pitched wails. With each bump and wail Albert and Pilot curse Ratso Sharpstein, the agent who sold them the Beagle HU-X2. It was pathetic and frightening just how bad the Stellarcraft Silverbird was turning out to be. At the same time Albert knows the fuel problem is not entirely The Beagle's fault! Someone (Not naming any names) forgot to top off the fuel cell before blast off. Truth is, Pilot apparently thought Albert was responsible for re-fueling... while Albert thought Pilot had it under control. Dahlia thought it was Terrier's responsibility. Ultimately no one checked. Each had forgotten to ask the other. Ordinarily it would not have been a problem, but as they were forced into so may energy sapping detours along the way that it was only after they were halfway through Orion's belt with 40.6% of the outer skins peeling away that Albert became aware of the problem.

The emergency holovid screen, trained to automatically expand and accommodate electrical surge, now displays slow motion arcs outside the ship. Albert runs from one side of the ship to the other to look out porthole visor stations. Despite their displeasure at the alarm siren, no one seems to know how to shut off. Long graceful green lines shimmer sunward across space emanating from planet Earth. His fellow crewmembers stand behind him watching.

"It's happening gentlemen," Albert sighs, "Just like I said it would. Mother Earth is coming into her milk."

"Okay, let's jump on this!" says Terrier, eyeing the space ship's nearly empty fuel indicator gauge. Terrier got his nickname from his schnauzer-like beard and feisty attitude.

"The converter...she'll fuel herself once we get down there. Watch and learn, gentlemen. Waaaaaaatch and learn!" says Albert in a know-it-all tone.

"I'm getting really sick of you saying that," says Pilot. "You watch and learn for a while ... and ... keep quiet while you're learning!"

"Okay Okay," says Albert, "Everybody just relax, please. In short order there's going to be so much energy floating around that we won't know what to do with it. Just free for the taking. Hell's Bells, in thirty days we'll be selling excess power on the panek-joreen market! We're rich, my friends! As they say on Earth ... filthy rich!"

Pilot sneers but keeps quiet. He hovers over the controls in front of a grey converter tube screen not yet used on this trip. He gently moves the joystick intended to relay back response co-ordinates to the thick puck-like cursor on the floyt screen.

"Now it's your turn to watch and learn, Mr. Albert. I will simply ... extend ... our converter tube. Easy! Easy! ... perfect! Then swing it around to port ... like so ... Easy! Easy! ... Perfect...piece of cake. Keep going ...

THIRTY-THREE

While Pilot maneuvers the space crane, a transparent striated hologram image of Earth floats just above Albert's screen. Bathed in a teal glow, the planet's oceans shimmer. Albert checks a large gauge on his wrist then says, "There are pulses around the planet's axis end. Not to worry. Zey are called northern lights ... a solar flare phenomena ... no big deal. But ordinarily we don't see that teal glow. I believe that's an indication of striate warp indicating the planet will soon enter spinneture!"

"And the criticals?" Terrier asks.

"I don't want to sprain ankles on anybody's parade, but those criticals don't look right to me," interrupts Pilot.

Pilot is proud to be the only Ein aboard authorized to wear and use the fard skin control helmet. His knee-high spat socks are interwoven with red coils which flash a pulse-rhythm reflective of his heartbeat called "Feet to the beat". Pilot's shoes look positively Turkish with their curly toe points ... the only form of relief he knows for his flat feet. Penny-white tri-lenses hang loosely around his neck ready for use. It is Pilot's job to navigate whenever the ship must travel through the dark and intricate wormholes of interstellar crawl space.

"Our criticals would be a lot better if "someone" hadn't forgotten to re-adjust the star post when we passed through Comet Wash," whines Albert.

"Give it a rest." Says Dahlia.

"Oh, So you never made a mistake?" says Pilot to Albert, "What about your Earth nuclear fiasco and that ... bird around your neck? Is that an award?"

These two periodically go at it. They get on each others nerves. But Dahlia again tries to cuts off their sniping, "Alright ... that's enough! Albert, what do the criticals read?

"They're saying everything is a go ... or NEARLY a go," says Albert.

"She's ready for milk, then?" asks Dahlia, the only female on the crew. She's not pretty in the conventional sense, but does have splendid long frizzy red hair and an aquiline hooked nose. Her detractors have compared her to a mynah bird. She was contracted for this trip because she is an experienced co-pilot and a highly educated space modalist.

"Any minute now she could start milk," says Albert.

For the reader's information, "Starting Milk is when a heavenly body begins oozing white-hot liquid iron energy from within its molten core after its millennium process begins. Pressure builds from the planet's central black hole's inverted gravitational relationship with time. Liquid iron energy (Milk) is totally different from magma. It is super hot and pure white. Planetary milk is squeezed from a heavenly body when time as ironized magma inside the planet inverts its elemental crystalline construct, and doubles mass with each inversion. The interval between inversion events is reduced by a half-life with each incident thus forcing the planet's mass to expand while its volume decreases. This compression of ironized magma into expelled milk collapses the planet further upon its central black hole. The now over stimulated black hole begins devouring the physical elements which define the planet; mountains, rivers and oceans ...and most important, as previously stated, it devours time. Scientists on the seven allied planets in Galaxy AK-47 were the first to realize that when a planet's component time elements are plugged into formulaic conservation of mass and energy laws... then and only then, can accurate predictions be made as to when a planet's time inversion event will occur. As all energy dealers in the Galaxy now know, only between the inversion event and conversion to black matter, can the energy ooze, called Milk, be harvested. This is still called the Einstein Feast and lasts only forty-eight hours after which there is real danger of increasing gravity sucking any unsecured spacecraft into the growing vortex.

THIRTY-FOUR

A message dances across Albert's computer screen ...

LOCKED ON TIME SEAM ... LOCKED ON TIME SEAM

This message is delivered in a pattern of exotic dia-
podric pctyls and is cause for celebration. The four Eins,
their wild hair standing on end with excitement dance.
Their wire-rimmed spectacles are misting from sweat.
Their noses flare. Albert pops a flomite of Borduu Bubbly.
Albert is a good dancer – something he picked up while at
Princeton University. He puts on a well-worn disk-O-let of
electro-forced primo beat porno music. Each Ein (except
Terrier) begins to gyrate spastically to small shocks which
white-arc across the room timed to the beat. Clocks on the
walls can only watch and roll their tails. Most clocks have
weak entrails and easily become ill with motion sickness.
Sometimes they'll try to take part in the fun, but today
they're too sick from turbulence to partake in the odd
mixture of joy and concern vacillating among the crew.

Alternating with the message ... LOCKED ON TIME
SEAM... LOCKED ON TIME SEAM ... is the flashing
warning ... ENERGY LEVEL CRITICLY LOW ... ENERGY
LEVEL CRITICLY LOW.

Amidst the excitement of wildwhisker dancing no one
notices the air-door to the cold room slide open. No one

159

sees the stiff-legged ice-encrusted Ein who staggers in. His face, hair, and beard are covered with frost. This Ein stops under the biggest noon-beam wheezing wall clock and stares at the revelers. His mouth is open in astonishment as he observes Albert holding both hands high demanding silence when the music stops. He watches and listens when Albert says, "Hear! Hear! A toast to Cashman Arachnal ... and even to Sharpstein."

"Yeah, Sharpstein the stinking deronimo!" shouts Terrier.

Laughter. Cheers all around.

Albert continues, "... and let's drink a toast to ourselves for making this adventure happen without significant problems! In a few days Earth's milk will run and if we re-fuel smoothly and get out of here in short order."

Terrier is the first to notice the intruder whose frost has mostly melted now revealing features he recognizes – the cucumber-like nose, the regal bearing. Those traits, along with the slack left arm sleeve make it all but certain this Ein is none other than the legendary...Torikk Commissioner.

It is not unusual for star freighters to take passengers on board whose bodies are delivered encapsulated, sealed, and pre-iced for journey. It is not unusual for an Ein as famous as The Commissioner to have only his family name printed in braille on his lanyard. In this case the name Roberto Rothsbanyo attached to his ice capsule would not necessarily alert crewmembers about the important occupant inside. The Commissioner is the sole paying passenger on this trip. And, yes, this IS the same Commissioner who was sent along with Abel to bring Albert Einstein back from Earth eighty-one years ago.

Now all the crew except Albert see The Commissioner and no one joins Albert in his toast. No one shouts, "Anbat Anbat Shabab!"

Albert looks around questioningly as the cabin experiences one of those odd moments of silence when, at the same time, everyone and everything goes quiet. Terrier alerts Albert by nodding in the direction where The Commissioner stands.

"Oh Jesus!" cries Albert fingering the albatross hologram hanging around his neck, "... Mr. Commissioner?"

The Commissioner, even more surprised at seeing Albert, vigorously brushes the remaining ice crystals from his face with his good appendage asking with true amazement, "... Albert Einstein?"

Turning to Ein-Pilot, the Commissioner demands, "What the fotch'n ra is HE doing here?"

"Uh ... I believe Cashman Arachnal hired him as kitchen staff, sir!" replies Pilot.

"What are you talking about?" asks The Commissioner.

"How do I explain? Let me see ... first Albert worked as the cook. Then ... well, it turns out we needed extra mind function with computer navigation after we experienced a slight ... uh ... course navigational mishap ... and, it's a damn good thing Cashman hired him because, as it turns out, Albert is quite knowledgeable about planet 890 KL!"

"Wait a minute. 890Kl? That's Planet Earth. What's Planet 890kl got to do with anything? We're supposed to be arriving in Alpha Centauria in S5 psi, " says The Commissioner.

"... sir ... well ... you see ... Albert is sort of an Earth expert?" says Dahlia.

"Is that so!" says The Commissioner, "And, would you please tell me why we are we even discussing Earth?"

Pilot responds, "Sir! Okay! While you were on ice ... uh ... we uh ... Terrier and I ... uh ... experienced a directional miss-read ... a pretty big one ... and ... we ... had to change course, sir. As a consequence we used more fuel than anticipated. That's why we are presently orbiting Earth ... because Earth is about to go millennium with an energy burst and give milk," explains Pilot.

The Commissioner is speechless. He stares at them each in turn. Finally he asks, "WE had to change course? We? Clue me fathomless, Captain Ahab, but I was under the assumption this starship was on its way to Alpha Centauria."

"Yes. That's true. We were ... and will be on our way again sir. Soon. But, while you were on ice we had a low energy problem." Said Pilot.

"You can't be serious," said The Commissioner.

"I regret to say that, yes, I am serious sir," continued Pilot, "But Albert here came up with a solution. Knowing that we needed to address our energy situation quickly, and because he knows Earth so well, he showed us how it would make sense to head toward Earth, which is about to express her milk, and refuel. We see no problem inserting electrolysis tubing into Earth's time seam before she milks ... to refuel, and then if things go according to plan we can be ...on...our...""

The Commissioner holds up his hand for Pilot to stop. He walks over to examine the blue-green planet displayed on the fully flared compuitilab screen.

"Is that Earth? Let me get this straight. Are you saying that we are presently orbiting Earth ... the same planet where this so-called "scientist" (pointing to Albert) did all his damage back ... what ... eighty years ago?" asks the Commissioner.

"Y ... y ... yes sir," Pilot stammers.

The Commissioner glares at Albert then says, "Alright, you listen to me now. I don't want there to be any mistake about this. I do not want some albatross-wearing convict having anything to do with my plans. And don't for one pound pressure think I don't see what's going on here. No way! It's not going to happen! WE ARE NOT GOING TO MAKE CONTACT DOWN THERE! Is that understood?"

"Oh, yes, of course not sir, but ..." says Albert.

"No 'buts'" snaps The Commissioner.

To the crew The Commissioner asks, "Isn't one of you idiots wearing the albatross enough? Do you all want to be brought up on charges?"

Stepping out of the Commissioner's glare path, Pilot hesitantly point-stabs his silver automated finger hologram at the flashing ship's fuel gauge. "Sir ... we're running on empty. We simply don't have a choice. You have my word, there will be no unnecessary contact."

The Commissioner pauses to inhale deeply from his nitro bag. He counts to ten. After exhaling the last of his fog onto his wristwatch he begins softly, reasonably, "I like your choice of words, Pilot. 'Unnecessary contact' That's good ... wise ... diplomatic even."

But The Commissioner's attempt to remain calm fails. His latent sexual anger pent up over half a century whips his words from his mouth like silver spadarrows, "Let's get something straight, Pilot, I did not come all this way to collect *energy time-rip Earth milk funds!* If you have problems with recall you can frisk the itinerary disc where you will see clearly that WE, or at least I … am on my way to Alpha Centauri where I am scheduled to meet with Amalgamation fathers with whom in twenty-one horologic compendia … I will be draining sinoid with the best and the brightest! Do my words compute?"

The Commissioner blows away any fog still surrounding his massive wristwatch before continuing, "Let me repeat myself … by twenty one horloge compendia … after we turn this crate around, WE WILL ARRIVE IN ALPHA CENTAURI!"

His face is thawed now and quite red with after-wash. He adds, "And since you know who I am … you must know THAT I BROKER NO NONSENSE. I am a fair man. And if you somehow are not aware that I am a loyal Torrikk who has worked his ass off for eighteen ye … "

But before The Commissioner can finish his boasting rant, the ship lurches violently. Clocks give a shrill collective gasp as suction cups squeeze and clench their junkers trying to hold them to the ship's walls. Torikk clocks are easily frightened and these are terrorized … their dials quiver. Time leaks from a few dribbling down the wall obscenely.

Pilot interrupts, "Sir! What you just felt … that's a vacuum bubble in a fuel cell. Those bumps are occurring frequently now… ever three quadrille. And, with all due respect, sir, not to disrespect you, but while you were on ice for the last thirteen years, your conservative party back home was hard at work embezzling everything that wasn't nailed down … including almost all available time-energy funds."

"I'm sure they had good reason," shoots back the Commissioner who is no stranger to deflecting political barbs.

But Pilot is angry, and despite his better judgment, says, "Well, if you consider endeavoring to prove that Adam Smith and Eve Longombardi's encounter with the nep-con Snake of Deceit in the proverbial apple orchard of Edenoktowabe' to be not only historically correct, but a deserving project for public money, to the order of 78% of the yearly energy budget, then, yes Sir, you certainly got our money's worth!"

The Commissioner has made a career of debate but he is not accustomed to contradiction or cynicism. Especially when it makes sense. Add to his discomfort the fact that his frontal lobes are still cold and pain him with periodic brain freeze. His brow furrowed, he studies Pilot before saying in a rather patronizing tone, "When you get to be my age and have seen what I have seen, you will realize things aren't always as simple as they seem, Pilot!"

But Pilot shoots back, "No sir. And to your point ... The snake in the garden, a fer-de-lance no doubt, who decided to implement your Conservative Liberty Party's trickle down economics "starve the beast" program, starved it until the whole amalgam economy is now stone broke, sir, busted, empty ... out of gas just like our ship ... sir!"

Pilot is angry. His face and beard glow red. It should be remembered that whenever Terrier or Dahlia joked about Pilot being the product of home schooling he would let them know he graduated top of his Space Pilot class and obtained his Ace Pilot's credentials after only five years post-dictum. Unlike his single-minded classmates, Pilot is well rounded in his studies. For two years he studied Psychology and wrote what many consider the definitive abstract on Dr. Parmer's work with mules. Parmer as you may remember, was the first to correlate similarities between Torikk's famous Broadaxe Mules and partially intact Torikk males (like The Commissioner who were failed products of the first psycho-deviator operations) Parmer documented these men's inability to back down from flawed positions while noting their brainwaves were nearly identical to Broadaxe Mules when given the command to back up.

Pilot, having aced contemporary Torikk history, is also aware from the extensive press coverage at the time, that only one of The Commissioners testicles was de-cavitated. This would mean The Commissioner retains one male irritant, and is still capable of violence at a moment's notice. In fact, studies showed an unintended result of the botched operations is for the remaining gonad to over-compensate. When stressed, it is capable of generating extraordinary levels of testosterone. This phenomenon is not all negative. In fact his high testosterone tolerance for pain and willingness to get down in the dirt and fight has seen The Commissioner through some very tight situations ... both for himself and for the entire Space-Nation of Torikk. On the negative side, The Commissioner smells bad and suffers terrible insomnia. This Commissioner would surely never admit it, but he is one of only a handful of men on Torikk who experience almost crippling bouts of lust from time to time. But here's the thing. The Commissioner is a proud man. Add to that, he is not ashamed of his pride. Worse yet, and he, again, would never admit it, but he actually enjoys acting pig-headed and closed-minded. It makes him feel like one of those Clint Eastwood cowboys in old Earth Westerns who are required to check their guns at the doors of fancy saloons. Only it isn't his gun The Commissioner is expected to check at the door, but his ability to be reasonable and dis-engage before entering political discussions. His testosterone enables him to ignore what he knows are legitimate points of view held by others so he can get away with acting like a prideful mule and continue wallowing in know-it-all male pontification. All this he does on one testicle.

"Look, I'm not here to argue politics with you clowns!" snarls the Commissioner, "There are laws about making contact down there ... laws with teeth. (fingering Albert's albatross crucifix) Albert, you should know this better than anyone. Christ almighty, are you stupid? The Amalgam passed those intellocator laws after YOU ruined life as they knew it on that pathetic little planet. You ... and your ... psycho-archeological mayhem (He Mimics a child) *Humans can handle nuclear power, yes they can. They seem intelligent and responsible enough for me! They'll never make nuclear weapons. Count on it!* Isn't that what you said?"

Albert mumbles inaudibly.

Pilot speaks up, "Sir ... in point of fact, you may be correct. But we still have a real problem on our hands. That planet down there ... with its blue seas and its ... green mountains ... and pink humans are doomed. If we stand by and do nothing ... if we do not milk off the angeoanylgynetic endocrinal energy ... energy we desperately need to get you to Alfa Centauri so you can get your ... medals or whatever, then sir, that planet and all its sweet life is going to ... very soon ... invert magnetics and suk-slip away without a whimper."

The Commissioner advances looking like he might literally bite Pilot's head. But only inches from Pilot's face he stops and stares into Pilot's false green compound eyes. The Commissioner can see his own uncertainty reflected back a hundred-fold. The Commissioner says, "Don't mess with me Pilot! Are you sure about this?"

But it's Dahlia who answers from across the room, "Take my word, Sir. Earth is going flat-line memorastatic in four days!"

THIRTY-FIVE

"**F**otch!" bellows the Commissioner. He accidentally kicks out a clock's support, "Oh sorry. I didn't mean that ... But, tzench, I should have known if I let you idiots ice me something like this would happen. I'll be damned if I'm going to miss the one event I've worked my entire life for. No way! We're leaving this orbit as fast we can reprogram out route source ... and that's final! Young lady, what's your name?"

"Dahlia, sir.""

"Will you please see to a directional change for me, Dahlia?"

But before Dahlia can try to extricate herself from this awkward situation, Pilot says, ""With all due respect, Sir, I am in charge of this ship. And if there was time for discussion concerning our energy situation I would be more than happy to accommodate you. But our situation has deteriorated beyond dire."

"Listen, if we need energy that bad I'll give you permission to use my personal credit coupon to borrow milk funds!"

"Borrow? Out here? Borrow from whom, sir? Ronald MacDonald?" asks Pilot.

Terrier hides a snicker behind his Foo-Manchu face hairs. Realizing that time has passed for trying to reason or ponder, Pilot gives a quick hand signal to Dahlia who taps the zeta keys on her wrist. For the first time in their lives they must use martial art skills they have trained for. It's important to note that Albert, Terrier, and Pilot (and Dahlia of course) had been testosterone free since infancy and have never committed a violent act in their entire lives.

The Commissioner, his finger pointing like Clint Eastwood at Terrier, stomps toward the smaller Ein flashing serious stink-eye. The Commissioner's mouth is open and about to unleash a string of invective when he is snagged by Pilot's curly toed shoe. Though dog-thin, Pilot's prosthetic leg is piston-slung and powerful. The Commissioner bellows as he falls. Dahlia screams with terror and excitement. Terrier cries out. While still screaming Dahlia jams a stick of tyrocydephin up The Commissioner's nose stopping all motor functions with a hiss of nitrogen pyride freeze gas. Dahlia then opens his britches hole and shoves a second stick up the quivering Commissioner's butt. After loosely runcible-gagging The Commissioner, Terrier binds his hands and feet with partridge tape. With freeze drying of his cortical membrane complete, Pilot now attaches two suitcase handles to The Commissioner's rigid back. Pilot and Terrier drag him back to the cooler.

THIRTY-SIX

P ilot wrestles with the controls. The Ein crew monitors their displays anxiously.

Terrier shouts, "Hey ... What the...? What's that ... that coil in the tube?"

Pilot scramble-scrolls a Cyclops eye along the outside of the ship. And there it is ... the tube. Almost immediately a bright light flashes.

Pilot shouts, "CUT THAT GODDAMNED TUBE! CUT IT!"

Terrier yanks the robo-palm, which has automatically dropped down from an outside derek. "It won't cut!" he cries.

"Oh Phatch! ... Phatch Phatch Phatch!" shouts Pilot.

Another large burst of light now sparks from where the energy-harvesting crane had been attached to the ship just moments ago. Large shards of glistening metal and debris fly off into space. Now the mangled tube is drifting away too leaving behind a fiery smoking hole in side of The Beagle HU-X2.

"Holy shit," says Dahlia.

RED ALERT-
ENERGY ON EMPTY
STRUCTURE COMPROMISED
STRUCTURE COMPROMISED
STRUCTURE COMPROMISED

RED ALERT–

The Ein-Aliens go into emergency 1 procedure strapping themselves in. They prepare for a hard landing.

Albert whispers to Dahlia almost inaudibly, "I've always wanted to go back."

Dahlia stares at him in disbelief as alarms scream and the ship lurches violently.

"We're going down!" shouts Albert.

THIRTY-SEVEN

Though sexually altered, Albert Einstein is deceptively strong. It's a good thing too because he and his crew need every ounce of strength to maneuver The Beagle HU-X2 through the turbulent Earth atmosphere. They automatically switch over to reserve fuel tanks. But using up reserves means there probably will not be enough fuel to both propel the ship and run anti-gravity controls at the same time. It's like driving a car with failed power steering.

While they careen through the first wisps of Earth's clouds Albert Searches for grid signal points emanating off the velocopter he'd been riding those eighty years ago when that very unfortunate incident took place.

(BTW and FYI – There is a picto of a newspaper clipping which Albert Einstein has kept in his profile for eighty years. It is the only news source to report Albert Einstein's story correctly and was written by a young man named Tom Keller...a part-time musician who interviewed Harold Adams for the Times Picayune. Keller's story, buried on page 7 reads as follows.) .... *"Albert Einstein, the father of the theory of relativity is reported to have died today April 18, 1955. Some in Louisiana claim Mr. Einstein was an agent from the planet Torikk. We at the Times do not usually report on outer space stories or ideas, but in this case there are some interesting facts and coincidences. There are some who say the man who died today is not the real Einstein and that the real Mr. Albert Einstein was captured and deported some ten years ago by inter-stellar police while Einstein was delivering a lecture on time at Tulane University.*

Albert mutters to himself, "If I can just find that stupid velocopter. It can't be far from here."

Albert has the tractor beam coordinates and is getting weak signals every so often. Dahlia sidles up beside him and asks, "But even if we find it, will it run after all this time?"

Outside the ship, heat suppression tiles glow red hot from friction. Some peel away flaming behind The Beagle like hot ice off a comet. They produce a high whistle only dogs and animals can hear. Together, Albert and Pilot guide the Beagle above the trees. Branches snap and scream as they scratch along the red-hot fuselage underbelly of The Beagle HU-X2. Leaves, branches and more than one squirrel smash against the glass screen as the ship careens over the home of Colonel Steve and Jimmy Disciple. It's only when they hover-glide above the wooded swamp behind Dog Bark Comfort that Albert hears the distinctive ping that can indicate only one thing ... the velocoper is directly below.

THIRTY-EIGHT

Harold Adams is the motorcycle cop who ran into Bella in New Orleans long time ago. He is still alive. He was known only as special agent Harold, in charge of the UFO unit of the New Orleans FBI for forty-six years. His mother, God rest her soul, had been a daredevil stuntwoman and Harold had grown up following in her footsteps. He escaped a dozen near-death experiences including that incident in New Orleans. He should be dead. But he is very much alive. And though old and infirm on some days, Harold tries to perform daily isometric exercises, even if only for five minutes. He eats a vegan diet and still manages to squeeze into his dark blue uniform on his birthday; the one with the bar codes and the eagle gripping the lightning bolt in one claw and a bunny in the other.

The left side of Harold's face is a mass of tag warts. They hang like leeches. He's been cutting them off for the last twenty years with a fingernail clipper, but they just grow back. 8% get infected. After three knee replacements he can barely walk unaided.

Sworn to secrecy more times than he can count by the Marine Corps, the FBI, Homeland Security, and the C.I.A. Harold learned to keep his mouth shut after the Keller interview. But that doesn't mean he can't follow E.T.A. events on the inter-department scanner he managed to squirrel away in his underdrawers the day they terminated him. Security marched him out. He is 94 years old now.

Lately his diabetes has been acting up and confines him to his Lay-Zi-Fella wheelchair in which he reclines in vibrator mode most nights parked out on his porch eyeing the heavens and tuned into flashing gamma rays bombarding Earth. It isn't a bad life.

The night of May 25 2025, Harold listens to Tchump's alien contact offer with bitter irony. He is too old to go after aliens now. Even the nighttime stars hold no hope for Harold. He may be alive, but his dreams are dead.

Harold's home health aide, a Jamaican Maroon Iraqi war vet named Charles Winston, notices Harold's hangdog look when he walks out on the porch an hour before midnight to wheel the old man inside. Charles too has seen Tchump on TV and guesses what the problem is.

Charles says, "Would you like some weed, boss?"

"That would be nice Charles. Thank you."

Charles says, "If anyone could get Mr. Tchump his damned alien ... it would have been you, boss. You'd have brought him a bag of em ... at least a dozen wonky alien Eins in the old days!"

Harold looks up in surprise, "Why thank you Charles ... but, yes ... I'm too old. I really am."

It was not uncommon for Charles to see the old man cry.

Harold says, "You know Charles ... in a way I really am entitled to that reward money. I'm not bragging, but I've given years of service to my country chasing Goddamn aliens and UFOs ... getting probed more times than I can count ... got scars to prove it. I sacrificed my Goddam health too when I got all smashed up there in New Orleans."

"You certainly did, boss!" says Charles passing the joint and smiling at the shriveled old man.

"And you know what, Charles?" Harold asks.

"What, boss?" asks Charles plumping up the old man's pillow.

"I'm going to get that money," says Harold.

"Good luck, sir," smiled Charles.

" And you know what else?" asks Harold.

"What else?" asks Charles raising his eyebrows.

"You are going to help me!"

THIRTY-NINE

Harold's life ambition after finishing his tour in the Marines was to become a UFO cop, a Galaxy-wide Wyatt Earp. He wanted all the respect and interstellar adventure that came with the job. He'd been recruited right out of high school, whisked off to a New Mexico facility for nine years of intense underground and desert training. After a successful deployment in The Dakotas, not far from Mt. Rushmore, he requested a station in New Orleans. Why? Because he was an amateur sax player. Not too bad either. The way Harold figured, he'd had to give up family and friends for his job. But he refused to walk away from his one love, music. His job required he blend into the human scenery. Fine! He was not even allowed a dog – too much emotional baggage they said. Fine again! Harold could deal with whatever they demanded. And basically he filled all the molds they wanted him to fill ... except when it came to his music. Through all those years monitoring the heavens and checking out so many UFO sightings he insisted on practicing his tenor sax. And ... they let him. It was always Harold's dream to study with Jelly Roll Morton, the New Orleans king of sax.

After waiting eight years, Harold's request for a transfer to The Big Easy came through. He'd been in town only six months and already sat wide-eyed through a dozen lessons with Mr. Ferdinand Joseph Lamothe Jelly Roll Morton. And guess what! The great Jelly Roll liked Harold's laid back style. At least he said he did. Why else would he invite Harold to play a set with him at Les Bonne Temps Roll Me if he didn't think Harold had what it took ... that certain *je ne sais crois*?

Harold's musical dream was on its way to becoming reality. His ship was coming in. He could see it on the horizon. But at the last minute, that ship veered away from the dock and sailed right on over the horizon. Maybe his ship ended up in China ... or Japan giving someone else his dreams. That was the day Albert crashed his Goddamn cycleunit and bent it all to Hell. Or had Harold crashed into Albert? Whatever. Was finding fault important? What is important is that Harold got so banged up he couldn't remember how it all went down. All he knew was that he'd lost 78% hearing in his right ear. The left one had turned purple-brown – might as well be tone-deaf. Harold was not dead. But his dream was. And ever since the accident he'd been dragging the ghost of his dreams behind him like a kid pulling a little red wagon lying on its side.

Is it any wonder Harold thought about getting even with that alien, Einstein? That's right ... alien! Harold knew it. The whole office knew it and did nothing about it. For years Harold fantasized killing him. So what he was a famous physicist. Harold knew him for what he was – a Goddamn fugitive, an alien opportunist. Gun, knife, poison, whatever it took. He'd get him. But they wouldn't let him. And when Einstein disappeared there had been no trail. He'd just disappeared off the face of the planet And, not that Harord needed any more reason to hate Albert Einstein, but that clown really did inflict great harm on planet Earth with his stupid bomb.

The New York Times reported that the mad Ein scientist died years ago. It was so obvious to Harold that the whole thing was made up. A pack of lies. As an FBI e.t. operative he'd develop a nose for these things. Harold was a rat terrier kind of guy. He was not guided by newspaper reports. Harold followed clues, hard facts. He was a blood simple, skin and semen collector. He'd known as early as a week after his release from the hospital that interplanetary politicians had sacrificed him for reasons he never understood. But Harold clung to his hope for revenge as a rehabilitation motivator. His need to get even with Albert Einstein helped him through years of repetitious painful sinew stretches and ice water tank-therapy. He just needed the slightest interplanetary trail to follow. That's all. But hope for that went cold when America plunged into the Korean War.

Now here was this new thing – this reward being offered by that mad man Tchump. Tchump must know something. He'd had run-ins with Tchump when little David was a spoiled snot-nose skinhead in his twenties running interference for his father's clock business. But Tchump had grown rich and powerful, too rich for Harold to nip at his heels.

Harold felt entitled to that reward, all right! By dint of his service to his country. He'd earned it by sacrificing his health, his music, and maybe even his sanity after all that probing! He was no more ashamed of getting probed than getting a colonoscopy. Very similar. Christ, he'd been probed more times than he could remember; especially during the fifties when the Russkies and aliens all got caught up in that endless cycle of retributive probing. Half the time you didn't know if it was an alien or a commie probing you. Harold's ass had looked like a Goddamned teenager's acne face! Thank God for Bag Balm.

His dream of revenge? It was not pretty. It involved getting that Einstein fella strapped to a probe table and letting the old bugger have it with the blue angel – or the electric "eel" as they used to call it at H.Q. These implements were based on a barbed probe dropped by that alien Abel. But Harold would take his time. Maybe he'd dip the tip in sand.

Harold looks up at Charles from his wheelchair. Charles is smiling his stiff little Jamaican "Put da lime in da coconut and drink it on up" fat lip smile. Charles says, "It's not too late boss. If anyone got the know-how it be you!"

FORTY

Harold drifts off again. He dreams he is sitting astride his cycle-unit. He's going 90. He can feel the wind on his face. In his dream Harold wears no helmet. Like so many times before in his dreams he pulls alongside the bearded bastard who rides his own copter-bike. Harold reaches out to grab the old man's beard and tries to pull. He wants to yank the thing so Goddamn hard it'll drag the alien off his machine. Harold wants to watch the bearded hippie skid along on his stupid face – wants to watch pavement and gravel grind off layers of putrid alien flesh. And when the old alien is motionless, unconscious in the street, Harold will harpoon him with electro prongs until he is rigid. He will attach suitcase handles to the bastard and cart him back to his house, which glows from security lights in the distance. Harold will punch in his security code that rolls back the 16-foot-tall chain-link fence gate through which he will drag his Ein prisoner to his "work chamber". He will turn the dial and hear the hiss from lowering the "work" table to the floor for easy positioning of the body. Carbon straps will wrap like snakes around the prisoner's legs and spread them wide. Too wide. Harold has meticulously maintained this "laboratory" for sixty years. Semper-fi!

Always in the past during this dream the old alien guns it and swerves out of reach. This time, though, Harold actually grabs a handful of wiry beard. He pulls hard! He's yelling ... he has him ... but ... but ...

Harold wakes with a start. Something big – something big and dark is gliding overhead. Yes, he can feel it. It's above the trees. He cries out to Charles. Despite his bad ears Harold can hear the unmistakable high whistle his ear was long ago trained to identify – a sound Harold hasn't heard in years. Yes! There it is again. He hears the gliding slo-mo whisperinjetson-whine above the treetops like some flying balloon elephant.

Harold drags himself to his Lay-Z chair. He starts to dress. He calls to Charles again who still doesn't hear. So Harold wheels himself down the hall to wake the old Jamaican who, as usual, has fallen asleep in front of the Zellyoft watching re-runs of Pedro's Punditry.

He whispers in Charles' ear, "Wake up! They're here!"

FORTY-ONE

Charles pushes Harold's Laz-E Crawler up the street. He hasn't seen Harold this excited in years. A car speeds toward them from behind with what appears to be a Jack Russell driving. Jimmy Disciple's Churchmobile brushes against the Laz-E crawler. The occupants are hardly aware they hit anything.

Harold's and Charles cries are swallowed by the night. They grab for purchase on the green steel 20th century bridge railing in the split second they have. But the railing is four inches thick and they cannot wrap their old hands around it. Even if they could, they are too old to hang on. Harold's momentum forces him into and between the railings. His Lay Z chair remains mashed up against the bridge's slats but his body slides over the rail and tumbles through the inky night. Harold's last thought is Jelly Roll Morton smiling at him while Harold plays tenor sax.

Charles too flies over top of the rail and off the bridge. Both splash into the black Mighty Mississippi River. But it's as if it never happened. It is heard by no one. Long ago, Homeland Security deleted all record of Harold's existence. Now turtles will eat the last physical evidence of his existence, bones and flesh. Charles's body will be found weeks later. But no one other than Harold ever gave one good Goddamn about Charles.

FORTY-TWO

From where Dahlia sits strapped into her prone-bias line she comforts the clocks as best she can while Pilot struggles against Earth's gravity. But he's a professional and with Albert's help puts the ship down within a hundred feet of where Mr. Jimmy Disciple and the kids covered the velocopter with a camouflage canvas tarp. It had been imperative the Eins find the copter and Pilot has come through. Until Earth releases lacto-fuel, the only way to possibly get enough energy when they re-launch The Beagle back into orbit will be by employing the small energy efficient velocopter to find and collect primitive time energy. That is, if the velocopter will run at all.

A brief explanation here –

On Planet Torikk, energy funds are harvested directly from time. Eins long ago discovered mass is time and time is energy. Harvesting time turns out to be easier than you might think. In the old days you harvested physical timepieces – clocks, electric clocks, grandfather clocks, alarm clocks, and especially wind-up kinetic clocks because they were the most common source of energy on planet Earth. The process is simple. Clocks are run backward before grinding them to a fine powder, mixed with urine and allowed to ferment overnight.

FORTY-THREE

Like Harold, Laphonso is awakened by the high whistle of The Beagle HU-X2 as it circles before settling into the swampy woods behind Bella's house. Laphonso trots to the back door and stands on his hind legs. He whines softly. When no one comes to let him out he looks around to be sure no one is looking and takes the doorknob in his mouth. He twists. The door opens.

FORTY-FOUR

The Beagle's door opens and a pneumatic stairway slides to the ground where its base adjusts. Laphonso trots to where he can watch from the bushes. Laphonso is no frivolous nuisance barker. Ignoring a rabbit wanting to play, Laphonso sees Albert peek out then give the ok hand signal for Dahlia, Terrier and Pilot to follow him inching down the stairs. They walk directly to the velocopter and in no time they have it uncovered. Laphonso watches as Terrier examines the cumblustor tube. He carefully massages bulbous cheek-like saddlebag sacs slung over each side of the mainframe. Terrier puts his ear to the shroud hoping to hear a telltale suck-wheeze. Nothing. Terrier injects a florinella mist into the scoops, touch-pressures ignition ... and waits. Nothing. Five seconds pass ... ten ... twenty seconds. Terrier frowns and mutters, "It's not going to happen!"

Laphonso watches Terrier put his tools back in their saddle-creel. Terrier is wrapping his last squeeze bag clamp in chamois when he stops and listens. Laphonso hears it before Terrier. Then Terrier hears the faint hum ... hears It build to a high whine.

Terrier and the Eins are smiling now.

"She's damaged ... and woefully out of whack, but she sure as Hell can be salvaged. Can someone please get me a roll of adhesive ion?" asks Terrier.

Dahlia unwraps the strip she pulls from her creel and hands it to Terrier. They function as a team. All the Eins begin handing Terrier tools as he calls for them.

"Pliental"

"Here you go."

"Needleo"

"Here you go."

"Tri-bar"

"Here you go."

"I think that should do it!"

FORTY-FIVE

While Terrier continues to work on fine adjustments, Albert, Pilot and Dahlia walk back to The Beagle HU-X2 to commence the back-breaking work of disguising those parts of the mother ship, The Beagle HU-X2 not covered by the camo-sheetwash film ... an essential which Lia had the good sense to bring along despite Albert's constant needling about weight limits and over-preparation. This while Albert totally forgot to bring undershorts. Being the only female on board has not been easy. Dahlia is different from the men even though they are hardly macho types having grown up testosterone free. Because she is female, she is less forgetful.

While The Ein male still prefers to dress in drab greys and browns, Dahlia is distinctly feminine in appearance. Unlike human females, Ein ladies wear the same colorful outfit every day. Once a woman settles into her style in her late teens, her print, cut, and style are always the same. Dahlia wears a bright red tropical print dress with a single oversize dahlia on the front. The Dahlia is her namesake. As you may or may not know, it is also the Mexican national flower and one of the few flowers that grows on both Torikk and Earth.

Albert has begun covering the Beagle with Oak boughs. Dahlia, however, has studied Earth's vegetation and reminds him that oak leaves will wilt in short order making the ship look like a pile of fresh-cut decaying brush. She informs Albert the ship should be covered with fir, hemlock and pine boughs because they resist wilting the longest. She corrects Albert without value judgment – without inflicting the slightest know-it-all attitude sting. This personality skill is now instilled early in all Torikk children.

FORTY-SIX

Terrier is tightening the last pinion screw when he hears wet breathing behind him. He freezes. He feels hot breath on his neck. Despite being testosterone free, his is well trained in Kwat-Zi defense. Though he does not want to fight, he will if threatened. He summons his energy and directs it to his short motor muscles for maximum quick thrust.

Then he spins with his arm raised in axfeller position (still holding the clam wrench) only to abort his swing when a black nose and two black eyes appear only inches from his face. Terrier is barely able to swallow his scream.

But before Terrier can do anything, Laphonso pushes the top of his head against Terrier's raised hand which holds the wrench. He is fishing for a caress.

Terrier sighs. And after several unsuccessful attempts at verbal communication including French and Lithuanian, Terrier holds out to Laphonso his julee space-squeak voice box loaded with the latest version of earth-speak. It is about the size of a Rolaids antacid pill. Laphonso cocks his head questioningly.

Terrier advances pushing his right ear forward while lowering the left. At the same time he opens his mouth wide showing how one inserts the device down the throat. Laphonso understands and swallows the julee space-speak voice box in one frighteningly quick gulp. Five non-irritating whisker-thin appendages slide out allowing the device to lodge in Laphonso's throat just below gag response receptors. As if by magic, communication ensues – haltingly at first, but approaching fluency within minutes.

Laphonso – Where you come from?

Terrier – A planet in Fard Galaxy called Torikk.

Laphonso –Why you here?

Terrier –We need get Fuel from your planet's milk.

Laphonso –I do not compute this.

Terrier –Not matter.

Laphonso –Do you throw ball?

Terrier – Do you want me to throw ball?

Laphonso – Yes.

Terrier – Okay. Later.

Laphonso –Will you kill and eat us?

Terrier – No.

Laphonso –What you eat?

Terrier – Chocolate nut bar.

Laphonso – Do you like animals?

Terrier –Not eat animals.

Terrier – Good.

Laphonso –I eat animals.

Terrier –We want find clocks. Will you can help find?

Laphonso –Yes.

Terrier – Good.

Laphonso and Terrier say pretty much all they have to say in less than a minute. They go to find the other Eins who are just finishing up camouflage operations. Terrier introduces Laphonnso. Dahlia explains to Laphonso their need to get the velocopter in running condition. She and Laphonso bond quickly.

"We need harvest wind -up clocks. They are best and easiest fuel source here on your planet," says Dahlia.

Laphonso nods. Dogs intrinsically understand the time / energy concept. But they instinctively despise clocks.

Terrier continues, "On Tariik we harvest time. We grow it on farms. Of course, the best time comes from clocks that grow wild. Does time not grow on trees here on your Galapagos?"

Laphonso shakes his head, no. He laughs then excuses himself.

"May I ask something?" asks Terrier.

Laphonso – "Yes."

Terrier – I notice you sniff muchly. You are an accomplished smeller I take it, yes?.

Laphonso – "Yes I am. Why you ask?"

Terrier –"Can you smell clocks?"

Laphonso – "I can."

Terrier –"Can you smell from clock long distance?"

Laphonso –"Does dog have fleas?"

Terrier – "not compute."

Laphonso pretends to scratch.

Terrier laughs –" You da man."

FORTY-SEVEN

Laphonso sleeps many hours in a day. Over the years while resting he has wondered about the origin of the phrase "Dog in the manger." Since meeting and communicating with the Eins, Laphonso wonders if there will be a "Dog in the Manger" role for him to play when a comprehensive dog history is written. He hopes his efforts in helping the Eins' hunt for windup clocks will be taken into account by "THE BIG DOG." It is very important for a dog he be recognized for loyalty. Loyalty is what great 'Dog in the Manger' dogs do.

Not all dogs are capable of smelling compressed time in wind-up clock mechanisms much less differentiate it from battery driven timepieces. Perhaps only a 'Dog in the Manger' can hear a clock tick or move forward one quartzal from a distance of a hundred yards.

For the first few days Laphonso has led the Eins on raids within a twenty-mile radius. Two Eins follow him slithering through woods, shrubs, and bushes always out of sight while two others follow on the velocopter overhead. Yes, the velocopter is fully functional. Like foxes, Eins can run for miles, their balance is akin to Native American ironworkers. Their M.O. once Laphonso locks onto a scent is for Laphonso to case out the target home or office during the middle of the day when people are working or away from their homes. Then if the coast is clear, The Dog in the Manger (as he now calls himself) will gain entrance through an unlocked door or window. He will open the back door for the Eins to enter and bag their clocks – which often involves eviscerating the timepiece and discarding the housing and cord etc.

Although the Ein gang of four plus dog work hard, their capture quota has not been enough. Some days they barely harvest more compressed potential time than the velocopter uses getting them around. Dahlia articulates it best, "We need an extreme actionable!"

But Albert is hesitant to up the ante because some years ago here on Earth it was on just such a clock raid that he was spotted and identified by Harold of The United Foreign Object Space Agency. That unfortunate meeting ended, as we know, in a terrible crash in New Orleans unraveling the whole Ein Earth presence and, of course, the loss of their velocopter.

But Albert is reasonable and finally agrees they should at least discuss increasing their efforts. And just when Albert is coming around Laphonso confesses he's getting uneasy about leading these crime boosts. Dogs feel guilt much more than humans or Eins.

It is Dahlia who convinces Laphonso with a belly rub while asking him, "Who's the best Doggie in the Manger? Who? Who? Ahhh who's the best doggie in the manger?"

FORTY-EIGHT

O ne of the great truisms Earthlings say is ... "What goes around ... comes around."

It comes from Yajnavalkya's observation in the 9th century BCE that the Earth rotates around the sun. He was killed and eaten for saying this and no one said it again for thousands of years until Copernicus around 1520. Jacques Cassini said what goes around comes around in 1722. He was talking about the moon. "What goes around comes around" is true for a lot of things, disease, karma, and people. People, in the sense that those from our past keep popping up. In this case, the Tchump Family has its fingerprints all over this story.

The Tchumps made their money back during the war. In 1945, Hans Banju Tchump got out of Germany just before the Allies came in. They would have strung him up for his involvement in all aspects of the Nazi regime. Hans Banju Tchump, the great German master-watchmaker, torturer, and murderer immigrated to America and opened one of America's first mega-stores called TCHUMP'S CLOCK WORLD. Tchump was the first to offer hundreds, then thousands of beautiful clocks for sale to the retail public at wholesale prices. TCHUMP CLOCK WORLD was an immediate success. On opening day there were strings of tiny German flags extending hundreds of yards out into the massive newly paved parking lot. Busloads of customers arrived from as far away as Miami. Subsequent Holiday extravaganzas at TCHUMP'S CLOCK WORLD became synonymous with Christmas in Louisiana. Hans trucked in snow and live reindeer and not one, but three jolly pink-cheeked white-bearded Santa Clause impersonators. His son David Tchump handed out free cheap toy imitation watches to all the children. Hans Banju practically invented the business loss leader. The mega-store called TCHUMP CLOCK WORLD was the stuff of legend. After TCHUMP CLOCK WORLD went corporate in 1948 they purchased one of the first private corporate planes and had the famous TCHUMP CLOCK WORLD dial painted large enough on the side you could read it from the ground.

But in 1949 Hans was blindsided by Timex. By 1960 most watches went battery. Hans maintained it was just a passing fad and continued to invest heavily in wind-up clock mechanisms he bought cheaply from Japan. Like so many corporate giants, Hans drowned in the myopia of his unwillingness to see the future. Unfortunately, the same day Hans Bidju Tchump was smugly predicting the end of battery operated watches, Casio was just coming out with their digital readout face with a calculator, alarm system, and a sign of the zodiac reader. Hans Banju Tchump's world all but collapsed. The once famous Christmas party became only a memory. The term BYOE (bring your own eggnog) came from TCHUMP CLOCK WORLD now being able to afford only empty paper cups. When TCHUMP CLOCK WORLD announced it would no longer be giving out free children's watches, the kids begged to stay home and play on their game watches. They complained that TCHUMP CLOCK WORLD 's Santas had bad breath. Kids will turn on you so fast it'll make your head spin.

The smart thing for Hans Banju would have been to sell off the giant one-acre warehouse and move to a smaller space. But Hans was old school and he held on.

He closed off whole areas of the store until all that remained open for business was a showroom the size of a small-town five and dime. He did have the good sense to sell off fifteen acres of property before the State took it by eminent domain. 90% of his parking lot now serves Blue Bayou Community College. To this day Hans refuses to believe the wind up clock is dead. Hans is rumored to be well over 100 years old and not 'all there'. Whenever asked he predicts a comeback "any day now." Make no mistake, Hans was a rich man in his day. He'd been frugal during the fat years and socked away millions. After the collapse of wind-up timepieces Hans still regularly attended estate auctions and jewelry store closeouts buying up wind up timepieces for pennies on the dollar. These timepieces, often still in their original boxes, he catalogued and to this day stores in the dimly lit cavernous cobwebbed recesses of the original TCHUMP CLOCK WORLD Emporium.

Here's the thing. (and don't quote me) Many see his son's recent purchase of Yosemite and Yellowstone and his public quest for someone to bring him an alien as a cheap attempt at getting public attention in hopes of seeing a bump in the Tchump stock price before he dumps his shares. Some say he and the Russian dictator, Puotyn, planned all along to work together toward world domination.

FORTY-NINE

Hans Budju Tchump Sr. still runs his ad to buy vintage wind-up timepieces. "Highest Prices Paid for old gold. We buy wind up watches and mantle clocks, rings, jewelry of all types!"

He still buys as much good old wind up gold watches as he can get his hands on. He says it's on account of the fine microscopic milling of the gold gears. He loves the intricate brushwork on the face dial that never fail to make the hairs on the Frog-faced man's thick liver-spotted neck stand erect. His eyes grow misty at memories of a bygone happier era as a child growing up in the Sudetenland. He'll stop what he's doing and talk about when he strolled down Main Street Small Town America with his little son Hans Jr. (now eighty years old and buying up America's National parks) in tow, recognized and admired.

Old man Tchump's life is not a bad life. "Don't cry for me, Argentina!" he'll say with a smile as he makes his rounds winding each timepiece he owns every morning. Listening to the tick tock he can tell you which of his clocks needs cleaning, adjusting, or oiling. Lightning could strike and the power could go out all over town. This would make Hans happy. He'll sit enjoying the beautiful tick tock of his thousand and one clocks flowing in and out of synchronicity. He once confessed to a priest that the very act of winding all his watches and clocks makes him forget the past and feel holy – like he is the "King of Time." The priest smiled and said he understood, confiding that, though prideful for a man of the cloth like himself, he sometimes sees himself as The King of Prayer.

FIFTY

Hours are spent planning and rehearsing for the big raid on TCHUMP CLOCK WORLD. Two times Laphonso wormed his way inside the TCHUMP CLOCK WORLD warehouse to reconnoiter. On these sorties he wore a GPS tracker and vidioplex collar. The Eins, being meticulous to a fault, plan every move.

Then ... it's go time!

Albert, wearing his normal oversized coke-bottle glasses, blue madras cargo shorts, and a Ralph Lauren Polo shirt, walks into the TCHUMP CLOCK WORLD lobby. He pretends he's shopping for a vintage automatic self-winding La Coultre watch and asks the old saleswoman questions only Hans Budju Tchump himself can answer. He knows she will have to excuse herself and go back to summon her boss from his man-cave office where most of the truly great antique timepieces are kept.

It's the truly great antique timepieces, which deliver the most energy.

THE PLAN

Part A – When sales room is left unattended Terrier joins Albert in vacated storefront salesroom. Fills bags and wagon with watches and clocks.

Part B – Pilot and Dahlia hit Hans's office as soon as old geezer leaves with clerk lady to come up front. Walk from front to back takes two minutes each way.

Part C – Laphonso opens the rear garage doors allowing access for their Penske rental truck. (An hour earlier the dude behind the rental counter had actually not recognized the name Albert Einstein on Albert's expired 90 year-old drivers license. The dude scratched bug bites on his neck while Albert signed the contract.)

Pilot and Dahlia score two moon-phase grandfather clocks as well as three WLRN Public Radio tote bags they fill with fine old watches. Dahlia, Terrier and Pilot load hundreds of pounds of watches and clocks before Hans and the clerk walk to the storefront. By that time, the Eins are driving calmly out through the Community College section of the parking lot ... past Carlo and Mrs. Powers who are chatting beside her Citroen.

Mrs. Powers asks Carlo, "Hey ... isn't that your dog in that truck with those people?"

Carlo often brings Laphonso to class (where he is a big hit) so Mrs. Powers and many students know him.

"No, I don't think so," replies Carlo, "He doesn't wander much. He's a good dog."

FIFTY-ONE

Fortunately the War on Drugs and its Neanderthal policy of punishing drug usage ended with Bernie Sanders being appointed attorney general. At least now drugs are regulated and infused with automatic antidotes so that overdose is rare.

Perhaps the most over-used and abused drug on the market is Sam Adams Valentine Ale – Cupid's Love Potion #9. This India Pale Ale, triple fermented with steamed broccoli extract is high in oxytocin (who knew?) This beer is loosely called love juice, one bottle of which gives the drinker the exquisite feeling he or she is deeply in love. Brain is close to being addicted to Sam Adams Valentine Ale Cupid's Love Potion #9. Two bottles and lover-boy is head over heels ga ga. Three bottles and he gets debilitating infatuation with some amorphous angelic she-animus. Unfortunately, with Sam Adams Love Potion #9 there can be a physical transference of infatuation to any nearby person. In other words, like in some Shakespeare play, anyone ... including any WRONG or inappropriate person can become the love object. This is not conjecture. There are documented cases. Fortunately the effect lasts no longer than five hours.

"I'm a big boy. I can handle it," says Brain whenever Slipper or The Hairy Colonizer asks him if he has a drug *problem*. In fact they've asked him so often he's taken to drinking Sam Adams Valentine Ale – Cupid's Love Potion

#9 by himself in his room. Lately though, on a nice day he'll sneak off in the woods with three bottles to enjoy a beautiful love-high with nature. He knows it's just synthetic romance. But he doesn't care.

As Shakespeare would have it, Brain's favorite spot to drink and free-fall into cupid's baby pink arms is in a leafy bower by a stream at the foot of a live oak tree not far from where the Beagle lies camouflaged.

For an hour Brain has made goo goo eyes at a tiny trillium. He has composed poems and sings them to the tiny flower. His eyes have been focused on this wee blossom and when he looks up, his vision is blurred for an instant ... the very instant Dahlia walks past carrying an old Swedish wooden clock. Brain lays cloudy eyes upon her, puppy love eyes. She does not see him.

Almost instantly Dahlia's frizzy red hair and her aquiline hooked nose captivate Brain. Ordinarily Brain does not find thick glasses attractive, but under the influence of Sam Adams Valentine Ale – Love Potion #9, he finds Dahlia irresistible. He does not act, though. He watches as she marches along the trail until disappearing into the woods. Is she real? It's not like Brain doesn't know he is under the influence. That's why, perhaps, he waits. But when he finally decides to follow her ... she is gone. Brain understands the very real possibility he was hallucinating. He chastises himself for his indulgence and vows to lay off the stuff.

But next day he is back.

FIFTY-TWO

Professor Powers' physics lecture is nearing conclusion. She says, "Unfortunately, many in the scientific community thought Einstein lost touch with reason after the terror and destruction resulting from his relativity theory ... not for energy and social benefit, but for building bombs. He disappeared from the scientific scene for quite a while before he died in 1955. (Bell rings) Okay, I'll see you all after the holidays!"

After the students file out Mrs. Powers gathers up her papers and heads to the Blue Bayou Community College parking lot – once the parking lot of the old TCHUMP CLOCK WORLD Plaza. She is unlocking her car ... a French Citroen DS, when Carlo approaches.

"Wow! Neat car! Looks like a space ship!" jokes Carlo.

She smiles and says. "This is a French car from the nineteen sixties. The car preferred by General Charles DE Gaulle."

"Cool," says Carlo. "Hey, by the way ... that time stuff you were talking about today. That was kinda neat."

"Yeah ... it's radical, right?" jokes Mrs. Powers.

"Radical, that's a word my Mom uses a lot. You didn't grow up in the sixties, did you?"

"No, Carlo ... Do the math! I missed the ... sixties by quite a few years."

"Right ... sorry ... stupid me," says Carlo into his camera while rapping the top of his head with his knuckles.

Mrs. P. steals a look at her reflection in the Citroen's window asking herself, *"The Sixties? Is he serious? Girl, if you want that husband of yours back, you better start paying attention to business!"*

She turns to Carlo and says, "Carlo, have you given any thought to taking some literature or history electives next semester ... maybe some ..."

"I ... I might be dropping out," Carlo interrupts.

"You're dropping out? Well, I hope you're at least going to finish up your independent film project. I went out on a limb to get that okayed for you ..." she says with genuine concern.

"I know you did ... but, I'm not sure I can do it now ... because I'll have to give back the eye-core-d to the AV department. I really appreciate your help ... but ..."

"Look, Carlo! I 'm not comfortable with one of my best students just quitting. How about this? What if I give you an incomplete and an extension. Then you can use the eye-core-d to finish up? Here! Here's my phone number ... anytime you need help, you just call. I want you to finish this. You keep working and whenever you have new work to show me ... you just call me and I'll grade it."

Carlo gives her a hug in his exuberance just as a Penske rental truck with the Eins and Laphonso in it speed past them in the parking lot.

That's when we hear her ask, ""Hey ... isn't that your dog in that truck with those people?"

Carlo replies, "No, I don't think so. He doesn't wander much. He's a good dog."

FIFTY-THREE

Like she does every day, Mrs. Powers wave-streams The Rev. Al show while driving home. By the time she's showered and had what she calls her "Sam Adams Stupid Cupid" cocktail she's ready to sit down and watch Pedro's Pundrity.

Not yet home she listens to The Rev. Al on her car playdio. Rev Al announces that Mr. Tchump has just increased his offer to ten million shares of one of his companies if someone – anyone would please bring him a genuine live-and-kicking alien.

Tchump says, "Now, some folks are sayin' aliens are worried I might harm them and that's why they're not coming forward. That is sooooooo not true! Listen, I'm saying to any alien out there–I just want to talk ... one on one. I guarantee it will be in your best interest. I am one very wealthy Earthling and I may just have that sweet something you've been looking for. I don't know what that is yet, but I have whole binders of women if you know what I mean. And I'm pretty sure you have something for me. Here on Earth one hand washes the other. You scratch my back I'll scratch yours. That's how we do business here."

Mrs. Powers can't help wondering aloud, "What would it be like living with a filthy rich man like that? Not sayin' I would ... but still ..."

FIFTY-FOUR

It goes on for three days, Brain lying in wait, intoxicated, smitten. His friends think his behavior is odd, but Brain is an odd duck, a weirdo, a nerd, a real character. And on the fourth day after staying up practically all night studying, Brain is lying in the woods in the morning already in la la land after three bottles of Cupid's Love Potion #9. He is lying in wait for the red haired beauty he has seen before passing along the path below...when he falls asleep.

Shortly after Brain nods off Dahlia comes along and spots something unusual in the woods. She drops to the ground in fear. She waits.

Nothing.

She peeks. She crawls to investigate and finds Brain asleep. Her curiosity about a real human who seems to be around her age gets the best of her. Let's not mince words here. Dahlia comes from a society where each and every man has had his psycho-deviator guriad complex removed at birth. Growing up, she and her girlfriends took out library books with pictures of male genitalia. They'd watched both g rated and x rated movies when they were nine, and by thirteen Dahlia had seen her first porn flick. Males on planet Torikk may not have much interest in women and sex, but the girls do. And, according to all the mothers, it's a problem.

So it should come as no surprise when Dahlia does what she does. First, she is practically dying of thirst so she takes just a tiny sip of Brain's half finished bottle of Sam Adams Valentine Ale – Cupid's Love Potion #9.

Whoah!

She takes another drink, then another. Then she drains the bottle like a star sailor on shore leave.

Then, and you probably guessed, slightly intoxicated ... and ever so gently she lifts Brain's prom dress. He is, of course, going commando. And where she gets the nerve to do what she does next no one will ever know. She touches his balls.

Brain sits bolt upright. Unlike other males his age Brain is a virgin. He didn't plan it that way. It just happened ... or didn't happen. And certainly no woman ever touched his junk before.

Dahlia scoots back. For a second she sees the absurdity of the situation but absurdity can be pleasant under the influence of Sam Adams Valentine Ale – Cupid's Love Potion #9. As quickly as they move away from each other they are mysteriously drawn forward until they are kissing passionately mouth to mouth-tongue to tongue.

They tear each other's garments away, she, his prom dress, he her butterfly skin. Neither of them is experienced enough to know how or what or why they are doing what they do. They just know their clumsy attempt at making love feels really really good.

FIFTY-FIVE

Carlo feels comfortable with Mrs. Powers. Their conversations are warm and informative. It's not unusual for her to stop by now to view Carlo's video footage for the extra credit project she assigned him. She's gone out of her way to arrange for Carlo to borrow the College's electron fluoroscope recorder in his quest to collect unique footage, which he'll assemble into a montage of positive images about physics and life.

She knocks on his door. Carlo invites her in. They are alone in Carlo's mother's house. He shows her to a comfortable couch and inserts what he thinks is his extra credit memory v-nail in the video-meister slot. But as luck would have it, what he actually inserts is an un-labeled xxx-rated hologram he'd picked up at a yard sale called "Sexy sluts slurp Sammy's cinnamon stick."

In the few seconds the machine is loading data after he clicks "Play" Carlo dashes into the kitchen to get two Tri-guava sodas from the fridg-o-later. The video starts to play before he returns with the drinks. Nearly ten seconds of the XXX-rated DVH have aired.

At first Mrs. Powers thinks what she's looking at is a bit odd. (It's actually an arty slo-mo close-up of Sammy's member in geyser mode.)

"Oh no no no ... I'm so sorry," Carlo says rushing to shut it off.

But Mrs. P says surprises Carlo saying, "Don't get all bent out of shape, Carlo. I've been around the horn. I've seen porn. I wasn't born yesterday. I'm married ... my husband ... all husbands have been known to watch porn now and then. He even got me to watch with him. But it's not my thing. Porn is a cruel fact women kinda have to accept."

"Right," says Carlo fumbling to set down the drinks and remove the wheel-drive hologram.

"Really! I can handle it," she laughs.

"I am so so sorry," he says again. Will he ever stop apologizing?

"Well, get over it. Let me tell you a little story. Back when I student taught high school I was assigned the unenviable task of teaching Sex Ed! Talk about your trial by fire! So, yes, I can handle it."

"I don't know what to say," Carlo stammers.

"Look, I don't get embarrassed easy after that teaching ordeal, okay?" she says.

Swallowing nervously, Carlo says, "I'm sorry. I guess I'm the one getting all red in the face. So ... you taught high school sex?"

"We didn't call it that, but yes, and I found it was easier when I set some ground rules," she says.

"Like what?" he asks genuinely curious.

"I told the kids anyone can ask any question, any time, about anything they want ... anything on their mind! And either me or someone in the class will try to answer it honestly."

"How'd that go?"

"First day I got no questions. We just looked at slides and anatomical diagrams. I actually learned a lot about my own body. Then the second day all Hell broke loose with questions. Kids had to take a number, you know, like at the deli counter. We never even got to cover the material I was supposed to teach; the rhythm method and abstinence. They just asked and asked and I just answered or the class answered. Turns out most of them knew a lot more than me," she said settling in more comfortably on her end of the couch.

"I mean, like what kind of questions?" asks Carlo knitting his hands behind his head nervously.

"You know what, Carlo? I like you a lot. Let's not go there," says Mrs. Powers smiling.

They look at one another. Her phone rings. She looks to see who it is then says, "Excuse me, Carlo, I have to take this ... It's my husband."

FIFTY-SIX

The Eins work furiously unloading mountain of clocks and watches. Forming a starfighter's haul line, they shuttle-pass clocks up to Albert who carefully feeds them into the ship's digester.

"In the old days, free-sailing out in the galaxy, we used to fuel many of the ships this way, " he says, "By hand ... one clock at a time. Every ship had a digester like this one, only bigger. We got pretty good at feeding in clocks and watches!"

Then Albert adds, "If you don't mind a little advice, guys, it's best to wind them to just before the breaking point ... then Dahlia, if you turn the dials so the hands are pointing toward Rumelia it's less painful for them. What's the matter with you today? You seem ...distracted."

Dahlia sighs, "Nothing. We still need more clocks. Do you think I should go back out?"

Looking at the DP gauge Terrier says, "We're not going to make it."

Dahlia has two large sweat stains under her arms, larger than any of the men's stains. She has not told anyone of her encounter with the human. She is appalled at how easy it has been to break interplanetary law exposing herself to a lifetime of wearing the albatross. But she can't help herself. She is beginning to understand what Earthling love songs are about.

Burned out clock bodies lay in a smoldering pile. A fog peculiar to ionized time hovers over The Beagle.

FIFTY-SEVEN

While the Eins rob TCHUMP CLOCK WORLD, Jimmy D pulls the camouflage tarp off a big orange International harvester school bus parked behind his house. He purchased the bus a year ago off eBay for only a couple hundred bucks. The bus came from the estate of a militiaman named John Cage. Before he died, Cage had painstakingly re-configured the interior, removing all the seats and welding re-bar and flat steel sheets constructing a giant Hav-a-Heart trap catching key deer around Big Pine Key in the Florida Keys. But, as fate would have it, pretty much all the younger members of Mike's family were city folks up North and were creeped out by the thing. They were anxious to sell it.

Metairie Mike had equipped the open end of the cage about two yards back from the driver with an overhead re-bar re-enforced sheet metal plate that slammed down trapping any ungulate unfortunate enough to step on the trigger. Peanut butter was the lure. It had been smeared on the steps and all the way to the back of the cage.

Cage incorporated his business under the name John Cage Industries back around Y2K. He believed in his product and paid a lot of money for one of the biggest exhibition booths at the National Rifle Association's world of violence fair held in Muskellunge Michigan inside the War Memorial. He drove all the way up there some 2000 miles and was assigned a booth between The Winnebago

Motor Home Co. and Piper Cub Sea Planes. His trap created quite a buzz including a live interview with Field And Stream's new T.V. channel.

Then, as luck would have it, everything went to Hell in a hand basket. A group of militant key deer huggers heard he was there, flew up and demonstrated in front of his booth. A scuffle broke out when a very nice older woman in the CARE FOR MINIATURE DEER league got her ear bit by a skinhead who was drunk on Jaegermeister. This made local TV news and hurt business. John Cage Industries never recovered despite picking up a government contract from the Bureau of Land Management to remove caribou from Badlands National Monument. Unfortunately that deal got cancelled during the recession. The Govt. did order and received one unit, which was never used and ended up the property of Jimmy Disciple in the e-bay surplus online auction.

Before it went under, John Cage Industries limped along on profits from a previous invention that was quite popular in Northern American States and Canada. This was sold under the name 'John Cage Deer Spear.' It was designed to bolt onto the front bumper of passenger cars and pick up trucks and used parts from the front-end loader on a tractor but instead of having a bucket it had a seven foot long steel spear. Something like a knight's lance. The concept was simple. Instead of trying to avoid hitting deer on highways and roads you actually tried to hit them. You aimed your car equipped with the spring-loaded Deer Spear. The deluxe model featured an electric amplified deer call to flush them out of the woods.

The radio jingle went, "Just press your horn button. You'll attract caribou, moose, and even wild mutton! Ain't tellin' you nuttin' ... you never knew."

Once the "target ungulate" was speared, you simply pulled a lever, which engaged the tractor front-end loader device to lift the speared "ungulate" and deposit his still bellowing carcass on a modified Thule roof rack. You hardly had to slow down. For a while these deer spears were all the rage. But it seemed like bad luck was always chasing John Cage. A reprobate high school dropout from Duluth mounted a deer spear on his homemade "technical" and drove through the World's Largest Shopping Mall in Bloomington Minn. skewering people and flipping them up onto his roof. Before he was gunned down at the Canadian border he'd speared a Pakistani Sikh, a Somali and a librarian. Lawsuits were filed. And, of course, harsh new anti deer spear regulations were passed.

Noting how similar the bus was to his little Hav-a-Heart traps – only 100 times bigger, Jimmy D bought it from the government online auction site on a whim of divine fate. At the time he purchased it he had no idea how useful this bus –trap would be. It was just looked really cool and he had to have it. And doesn't The Lord work in wondrous ways?

While oiling gears and pulleys Jimmy D looks skyward. He whispers, "Thank you, Lord!"

Standing outside the trapping bus he gingerly pokes a hockey stick through one of the blackened windows to press down on the floor platform-trigger. WHAM! The iron barred gate comes crashing down and locks. Praise Jesus, it works like a charm.

Now to catch an alien! Jimmy D does his homework. When he keys in 'alien bait' on Google search he gets some startling information. Pretty much all aliens use clocks to produce energy in a pinch. CLOCKS! Who knew? Fancy old wind up clocks in particular. So Jimmy D spends the better part of the afternoon rounding up old clocks and placing them as bait in his giant Hav-a-hart Bus Trap.

Jimmy heaves a happy sigh and crosses himself. He throws Pedro up onto the bus dashboard, hops in and fires up the old diesel. She purrs like a kitten. With the newest root-rock-rap reggae version of Onward Christian Soldiers blaring from new Bose speakers Jimmy D installed, he grinds into first gear and lumbers off toward Dog Bark Manor.

FIFTY-EIGHT

Celebration is in the air. The Eins have nearly all the clock energy they need. Terrier beams. Her crewmates think Dahlia's open-mouthed elation is for the clock achievement, not that of a lovesick red-haired girl. The Beagle HU-X2 has only 50,000 PSI (400 clocks) to go until theoretically it will be able to launch and hover. From an orbit 187 miles above Earth The Beagle will be in prime position to harvest milk. Pilot is so pleased after making energy-crit that he agrees when Dahlia suggests they thaw out The Commissioner. Albert is against it but compromises at Dahlia's suggestion they keep The Commissioner at half chill.

Laphonso barks the all clear. The Ein crew emerges from where the Beagle HU-X2 is hidden in the woods. Terrier, Albert and Pilot hop onto the sidewalk for one last heist. Laphonso has alerted them of a cache of clocks in a school bus not that far away. They hear Dahlia overhead in the velocopter which Terrier has equipped with a crude sky sled giving an additional carrying capacity of nearly four hundred pounds.

Not two blocks later, Laphonso trots proudly toward an orange school bus parked in front of Mildred Peters house in the middle of the block. Grampa Joe has scandalized the town recently by moving in with her. She is transgender. Everyone speculates about what they might do together in the dark.

The scent of clock is clear to Laphonso ... old wood, wound springs, watch oil! It's all there! In hindsight the darkened windows should have tipped one of them off that something was fishy. But seeing Laphonso sitting in front of the bus door panting, the Eins approach.

Finally Pilot notices the darkened windows and warns them to stop. Something's not right.

"What's the problem? It's a goddamned school bus, for Christ sake!" says Albert knocking confidently on the bus door, "Watch and learn!"

He knocks again. When no one answers he motions Pilot to check the driver side. Dahlia lands the velocopter and sled behind Mildred Peters' forsythia bush. When Terrier gets the nod from Laphonso he signals "all clear" to Albert who gingerly pushes the bus door open ... slowly ... slowly.

Albert is met by the sweet aroma of old clock and watch oil. He gives the thumbs up and motions the others to follow him up the short bus steps. As they file toward the back of the darkened interior Albert hesitates. Terrier walks into his back and Dahlia walks into Terrier's back. They stumble and fall atop four French mantle clocks still inside their original 15th century sandalwood boxes.

"Oh Mammmaaa! Papa's home!" exclaims Albert fondling an Italianate clock depicting Venice and gondoliers on finials.

At that moment the repurposed Singer sewing machine treadle trigger unleashes the steel door behind them to slam shut entrapping all four Eins.

Almost immediately Jimmy Disciple approaches the bus from behind Mrs. Peters' garage. He cannot believe his luck. He must truly be one of God's favorites. It has only been three hours since he baited the trap. He opens the door and tosses Pedro up on the dashboard. He cannot see his captives because of the galvanized sheet metal wall, which has dropped. But he hears them moving.

Softly singing Leonard Cohen's *Hallelujah*, Jimmy D fires up the old diesel, wrestles the black floor stick-shifter knob into first gear, and lumbers away. Laphonso runs home.

FIFTY-NINE

What is wrong with you, dog?" asks Slipper, "You've been whining like crazy and twirling in mad circles since you came in the house."

"Hello! He's a dog. Do you speak dog?" asks Brain sarcastically, "He probably just wants to hump a rabbit or something. Let him out."

"He just came in. Maybe he's trying to tell us something," says Slipper.

"Oh yeah, like Lassie telling Little Timmy the bad guys got his mother tied to a bed and he wants Timmy to follow him. Or ... what's the other one ... Rin Tin Tin ... saw some hostile Indians."

"I think he wants me to follow him," says Slipper.

"You're really nuts," says Brain.

But Slipper does follow Laphonso and she grows even more concerned when he ignores a rabbit in his path. Laphonso leads her to where the bus was parked. But it's gone. Laphonso tries to follow the bus odor, but diesel fumes along with a myriad of other traffic smells foul and confound his nose. There remains only trace clock smells ... not enough to follow.

"What is it Laphonso?" Slipper asks.

She knows Laphonso is no flibbertigibbet! He's a serious dog. He would not go to all this trouble to bring her out here just to retrieve a tennis ball from a rain gutter or some such nonsense. But he can show her nothing but a hangdog look. Worst of all, when he tries to use the translator in his throat he only whines and whimpers. After a few minutes Grampa Joe comes out of Mrs. Peters house, saying, "If'n y'all be looking for that bus was parked here, it took off a while ago."

"That must be what Laphonso wants. Do you know who they were or where they went?" asks Slipper.

"Nope! Fer as I kin tell there was a bunch a illegal aliens got in thet bus first ... then that religious fella ... the one who bought the piece of junk from you kids, He got in an drove off. Did he ever come back for that thang?"

"Nope ... still there far as I know," says Slipper, "Anyway ... guess we'll be going. See you later Grampa Joe."

Slipper and Laphonso walk back home. Slipper is concerned when Laphonso ignores a rabbit along the way.

SIXTY

Jimmy Disciple and Colonel Steve hatch a plan.
STEP 1 – Fasten air vents to the bus roof.

STEP 2 – Rent a backhoe. Dig trench in back yard big enough to drive bus in.

(Colonel Steve rents a backhoe to dig the trench but hits water before going deep enough to completely bury the bus. The backhoe cannot dig and bury the bus deeper than its blacked out windows. The ground water level reaches the top of the bus tires making it damp inside the bus but there is little water incursion.

STEP 3 – Backfill and bury bus.

STEP 4 – Contact Tchump via false double blind servers informing him that aliens have been captured.

STEP 5 –Demand from Tchump a reward 4 times the reward offered since they caught 4 aliens.

After burying the bus and emailing Tchump Jimmy D., Colonel Steve, and Pedro set off in the Churchmobile to deliver the day's rabbit catch after which they go out for Mexican food to celebrate. Things are going well.

SIXTY-ONE

Birds everywhere fly up in the air just before a wave of strong tremors rocks the Earth. Dogs howl and whine. A second even more violent trembler hits. The shocks have been coming regularly all day. Small anthill shaped volcanoes form. They are from two feet to six feet tall. They hiss and gargle liquid iron like hot mouthwash.

Ash and hardening lava which pile up around the school bus air vents make it difficult for the Eins to breathe.

"I'm sorry guys!" coughs Albert, "This is all my fault!"

"It's not your fault," coughs Dahlia. "This planet is cursed."

Terrier has moved little in the last five minutes. His asthma has tired him to the bone.

At Albert's suggestion they form a vibration circle around Terrier and hold hands while meditating good intentions. But one by one they topple to the damp floor from lack of oxygen.

SIXTY-TWO

The Eins are not moving. Their expressions are those of the damned. Before he loses consciousness, Albert tries to beg forgiveness from his friends admitting that he's messed things up royally.

He whispers, "Again I've made others pay the price for my arrogance ... the ultimate price this time. I deserve this albatross around my neck."

Once again others will die – not the ungodly number like back in August 1945 when 200 thousand died the day the bomb was dropped. Who knows how many over the years suffered from the effects of Albert's bomb.

The Eins lay splayed on the bus floor. They don't hear Slipper's, Carlo's, and The Hairy Colonizer's running footsteps. They are too far-gone to hear pounding on the school bus door. The Eins do not hear when Carlo kicks open the bus door. They are unaware of Laphonso bursting inside brushing past Carlo and The Hairy Colonizer. Slipper figures out how to lift the trap's sheet metal wall.

The Eins do feel fresh air rushing into the sealed tomb.

SIXTY-THREE

Slipper shines her flashlight on Terrier lying in the murky darkness. She drops to her knees. She has been taking nursing courses up at the college and has volunteered weekends in high school with a certified veterinarian. She knows enough to be dangerous. She removes Terrier's helmet and touches his cold lips. Cold is not good. Using her index finger like a wooden ice cream spoon, she digs a thick slimy flem-ash lump from Terrier's larynx and flings it into the dark. Without hesitation she presses her lips to his cold whiskered mouth administering mouth-to-mouth resuscitation. Her breath enters his lungs giving him life. Love is the last thing she expects.

Terrier has been and still is in near-death rapture looking down from heaven where, in soft wonder he has been flying toward a big throbbing white light. Then ... where did it come from, the wet kiss? He never in his wildest dreams, which these may be, expects the hot wet mouth of God to clamp over his and blow humid girl air down his throat. The last thing he expects is to fall in love, but love happens, doesn't it. He tastes it. She tastes it.

Using his teeth, The Dog In The Manger drags Albert outside then scampers back in to help Slipper and The Hairy Colonizer drag Terrier and Pilot out. At some point here it becomes clear that Laphonso is, indeed, the Dog in the manger.

SIXTY-FOUR

Colonel Steven Golub-Singh has worked hard to be well-liked and well-connected in the community. He is wealthy and has given the town a yoga center with no strings attached. This has endeared him to the liberal ladies. His yogurt tasting parties add to his popularity. Some call them smash hits. So it comes as no surprise when after Googling the Colonel, Tchump says he will drive out to inspect the aliens which Colonel Steven Golub-Singh has supposedly captured. And, of course the liberal ladies all say that if anyone can catch one of these aliens, it's our Colonel Steven Golub-Singh. Colonel Steve has invited the whole neighborhood to welcome Tchump's entourage.

They wait. The ladies grumble. To appease his guests Colonel Steve and Jimmy D serve vanilla, blueberry and chocolate yogurt. Tchump is over an hour late when his limo finally arrives amid an entourage of reporters at the site of the buried bus. Jimmy D will present one of his famous Jimmy-Boy Bibles to Mr. Tchump. But neither the good Colonel Steve nor Jimmy D. has bothered to check inside the bus. Apparently each thinks the other has done it.

SIXTY-FIVE

In the middle school cafeteria a town meeting is in session. Citizens are visibly upset over a recent rash of thefts. Specifically, and this makes no sense to anyone, clock thefts. The older citizens make no secret that they suspect – aliens of the illegal Mexican stripe.

Because Bella has recently been elected president of the Chamber of commerce, she chairs the meeting. Bear waits outside.

She bangs her gavel. "Okay, I call this meeting to order. Today we ..."

But she is immediately interrupted by Grampa Joe wearing seersucker pants and plaid short sleeve shirt muttering through his food encrusted white beard, "Shit or get off the pot, Bella! It's drugs. I'm telling you it's aliens selling drugs!"

Bella is pretty good at handling these kinds of situations. She smiles and says, "Let's not go jumping to conclusions! My experience as a businesswoman tells me to wait until we've got all the facts. And even then ... proceed with caution."

A red-necked man wearing a grease stained dark green shirt and a baseball cap shouts, "I seen em sneaking around at night like rats!"

"You personally saw them?" asks Bella.

"Yup! I seen em! Or at least Tom down at Bears and Bombs Gun Shop did. Tell em Tom!"

"I seen em just yesterday!" says the man dressed all in camo who must be Tom.

"I seen em driving around in one of them hippie busses … an old school bus! That girl who lives with you … she seen 'em too. She was there with that ugly dog of yours!" said Grampa Joe.

A middle-aged Mexican man named Gomez says, "Seems like we got some other important problems here … rabbit problems. This town got more rabbits than the plague got rats."

An older white haired lady shouts at Gomez, "Rabbits don't steal clocks, Senor'!"

Bella senses decorum getting away from her. She cannot see who says it, but she clearly hears the shrill cry, "It's Mexicans what're stealin' our clocks!"

Everyone begins shouting.

Bella bangs her gavel, "Now just everybody hold on. I think what I'm hearing is that we've got a problem on our hands. Is that right?"

A bone-thin older gentleman with shirt buttoned all the way to the top of his neck. He sports a pair of grey Dr. Scholl's high tops with Velcro closures on his feet. He says in a shaky voice, "I just want to know one thing. Why is it you wet backs think it's okay to go around takin' people's clocks? I don't get it. Christ almighty Jesus, y'all don't hardly never use the clocks ya got! Hell, y'all er always late!"

A large woman in a colorful Mexican dress stands up. Irate, she shouts, "More likely some gringo going around taking clocks so you pasty-face Honchos can cheat us out of our work hours and pay less wages! You ask me, it's

Goddam Gringo cheapskates taking the clocks! That's what I think!"

A businessman shouts, "I don't know what's going on or who did it, but someone stole my time-clock ... ripped it right off the wall ... time cards and everything! Left a big mess."

His wife adds, "My husband's afraid to say it, but I'm not. It's Mexicans all right! How do I know? Because Chicanos always got dogs with em ... and some black dog did his business on the driveway when they was running out with the time clock!"

At that moment Sheriff Festus LaBoef lumbers in. Behind him he's pulling a child's Rapid Flyer wagon. It's hand-painted green and grey camouflage. He bends down and whispers in Bella's ear. In the audience some pushing and shoving is going on.

Bella bangs her gavel and shouts, "Hey! Hey! Fighting isn't going to solve anything. You want to fight? Go outside in the parking lot and fight. Look, we have a real problem here. Getting all excited and hollering at one another won't accomplish jackshit!! (gasp from the audience) That's right. I'm sorry I used a bad word. Christ, I don't know what words are bad anymore. Maybe you do. Just...everybody calm down now and listen to the sheriff here."

Sheriff LaBoef looks around for the microphone.

"There is no microphone," Bella whispers.

Sheriff LaBoef looks out over the audience, hitches his trousers up over his fat belly, then begins in his deep commanding military voice of which he is very proud, "Okay, folks. Y'all know why I'm here. Someone goin' around stealin' clocks. Bill, I heard you lost a clock that was very dear to your heart. (Bill nods) We all lost clocks ... family clocks ... clocks that meant a lot to us. Clocks that, to a degree define who we are as a community, where we came from, and what we stand for as Americans. These are clocks that can never be replaced."

Bill rises from his folding metal chair and says, "If I could I'd just like to take a minute and tell y'all a little something about my clock!"

Confusion follows. Seems everyone wants to talk about their missing clocks.

The Sheriff has to interrupt Bill, "Okay, Bill. Everyone's going to get their turn. I promise. Helen, you're next. Tom, you go after Helen, then Rosa ... "

Bill continues, "You know, my clock might've looked to some folks like just any old ordinary clock. Nothin special. But she ... I liked to call her a she ... because she was a gift to President Lincoln from his physician, Doctor Emery Richardson who give it to the President after Richardson's wife died of influenza. Emery Richardson's father brought that clock all the way from Stockholm Sweden a hundred fifty years ago on what was called the great Herring Boat Crossing."

The floodgates open and the stories pour out. It goes on and on, one octogenarian after the next. Many including Grampa Joe wipe tears from their eyes.

The sheriff is not a patient man. He'll put up with only so much useless gab. He grabs Bella's gavel and bangs for silence. "Listen up, folks. We could sit here and tell your old crappy clock stories all night. But we got a situation here! It's time to stand up and motivate! You men. Tom! Pete, Gerry, Bill, Gomez ... yer all deputized! Now listen to me!

You're part of the long blue line now ... a line of brothers. No matter what goes down, we share the code of silence, capisce?"

This is what they came for. They murmur agreement.

Outside they hear what sounds like the world exploding. The floor beneath them shakes.

Then it stops.

Grampa Joe asks, "Do we get guns, Sheriff?"

"You bet your ass, you get guns!" answers Tom the arms dealer nodding at the sheriff who is already bent over unloading AK47 semi-automatic rifles with drum clips from the wooden crate he was hauling in the Rapid Flyer wagon.

Surprisingly well armed, the citizens of Bayou Cheine leave the meeting hall invigorated. They bolster their courage at their trucks with rum and moonshine. Some prefer vodka. Bella remains behind. Alone now, she is thinking about Lenny. All those memories she's kept bottled up these last years have come out; memories like the first time they kissed; memories like home birthing Carlo where he'd gotten stuck in her birth canal and Lenny'd had to pull Baby Carlo's large purple head out with his bare hands.

Lost in memory Bella gets up and gathers her things.

"That went well," says Bear.

Bella ignores Bear's sarcasm and the two begin walking home. She laughs out loud as she tells Bear about her thirtieth birthday party where Lenny had an Atomic Neon Cajun burger shipped in overnight for her.

"Only...somehow the thing never arrived. Perhaps it's still out there," she says realizing how lucky she is to have Carlo and his friends living with her. How do people do it on their own? She is not really paying attention as she walks and nearly collides with a man walking toward her. These two walkers would have passed like comets in the night had The Commissioner not stumbled when passing Bella on account of his still half-frozen numb knees. Instinctively she and Bear grab his good arm to steady him.

"I'm so sorry, " the man says.

Bella is under the impression she knows everyone in town. This fellow is on the short side but manly in an odd way. She can't tell weather he just walks funny or is disoriented. Is he staggering? Drunk? Upon further study she sees he has no left arm filling the sleeve of his strange shimmering uniform.

Still suffering from the effects of being on ice for months, The Commissioner manages to produce a contorted smile for Bella. He is not practiced in the art of smiling and continues working his lips nervously. He passes his right hand through his long frizzy hair. His fingers catch where ice crystals and dust have formed snarls and hair knots like on a dog's fur.

Squeezing his muscled arm in her hand Bella experiences an odd almost electric current of excitement – as if someone dunked her hand in a bowl of hot soup. Suddenly The Commissioner who had been chilled to the bone for months... is sweating. They both are aware something magical is happening. Their meeting has become some kind of cosmic flowering. And neither of them has had a drop of Sam Adams Valentine Ale – Cupid's Love Potion #9

They're giddy. The hair on Bella's neck stands straight out. Her nose sweats. Follicles on her head ooze hot oily pheromones making her scalp tingle. She scratches the itching on the top of her head. Between these two strangers a static amperage arc-zigzags back and forth like between two Tesla points causing their eyes to dilate wider than oyster shell buttons seeded with blueberry pearls. Photons sparkle on the tips of Bella's eyelids and eyebrow hairs. Puffs of golden breath dart like porcupine quills dipped in liquid nitrogen from The Commissioner's tongue as he speaks. The electric quills pierce Bella's lips, her cheeks, her chin. Bella cannot take her eyes off his mouth. She is in love with him... loves the curve of his lips and the tip of his tongue, which protrudes slightly and rests seductively slippery with saliva on his lower lip. She is confounded by The Commissioner's kind eyes. He is the most ruggedly handsome man she has ever met ... excluding Lenny.

For his part, The Commissioner experiences a polar-axis re-alignment brought on by female propinquity. Bella's ruby red grapefruit lips, her warm radiance, her soft aged spray-coat of melted camembert skin invites him to ...to do what? Kiss her? Really? At his age? He just met this Earthling. He's known her for less that a pfargo. She is forbidden fruit. And he's thinking of kissing her?

He has never married ... never even really dated. He chose celibacy. Back home many attractive women have hit on him throughout his life. He was never interested. But now... He is so totally unprepared for this ... this Earth magic. He thinks he might faint. Bella also thinks she might faint. Each reaches for the other to steady themselves. Really?

Their hands touch. A fine yellow down of Bella's arms vibrates sympathetically with The Commissioner's brilliant copper-red forearm hair. Without knowing or even caring why, Bella presses her oily perspiring nose to the skin just above his wrist. She inhales his intoxicating nutty man stink. Like a puppet's head on strings her head rises up toward his ... closer, closer until their lips, like two powerful cosmic space-ship refrigerator magnets, barely touch.

Janice would recognize what is happening here. It is the fundamental calling of bacteria ... the sharing of bacterial souls ... a connecting across the great coded saliva rainbow spacebridge. Their mouth liquids, spits, and papillae churn in Holy oral communion like amyloid enzymes as their tongues begin a dance, a cosmic minuet... the miracle of universal desire to procreate.

Later Bella will try to describe her feelings for her girlfriends. One friend loves her poetic description of feeling like a tomato seed in a peat moss love bed ... two kids in a tire swing over a summer pond. Her sourpuss friend Alice – not so much. Let it be known that Bella is the first woman The Commissioner has ever kissed. He'd thought about kissing Lola. But that was so long ago. The opportunity never returned.

Later, when asked, The Commissioner is not ashamed to say that his single testicle swelled to the size of a sweet potato.

SIXTY-SIX

Jimmy D. is holding Pedro and standing proud. Beside him, his lover, Colonel Steve Golub-Singh beams at the crowd surrounding the orange school bus – a crowd of at least forty murmuring townsfolk and reporters awaiting the arrival of Tchump. The rear door of the bus is secured by a heavy bronze padlock. A local doctor runs to the door and applies his stethoscope. He listens intently. He gives a thumbs-up.

Colonel Steve Golub-Singh ordered that foot long brass key made from True-Value hardware just for the occasion. This key hangs round his neck on a solid gold chain that's easily worth a thousand dollars. His Injustani heritage has instilled in him the importance of using gold to show people like Tchump they aren't the only high rollers in town. Who knows where a connection like this might lead.

He hears Tchump's motorcade arrive. With much fanfare, flunkies bring a ramp to the door of Tchump's double-stretch limo. The mogul glides down seated in his Lay-Z-Boy Scoot and motors over to where Colonel Steve, Jimmy D, and Pedro beam their most sincere smiles. After they shake hands and pose for pictures, Colonel Steven Golub-Singh holds high the giant gold key for public approval and photo-ops before unlocking the bus door. He is so slow that Mr. Tchump wheels past him. Tchump has been anxiously waiting this moment. He imagines aliens staggering out rubbing their compound eyes or eyestalks, or

251

whatever visual organs they might have. And even though Tchump has been told Jimmy Disciple provided three large porcelain potties with lids for sanitation, Tchump holds his nose bracing against any rank outer space smell.

He is not expecting the fetid smell of rabbits. Fourteen rabbits have taken refuge in the bus from violent earth tremors. They dart out now dodging around Tchump's wheel chair and run into the woods. Mr. Tchump, as everyone knows, is not into fun. He has a notorious temper. In a trice the old man is up out of his wheelchair railing against Colonel Steve Golub-Singh. His gnarled hands search for the Colonel's throat. Jimmy D rushes over to pull his lover out of harms way just as the Earth beneath them begins quaking so violently many in the crowd fall down. A great groan echoes planet-wide. All who survive tell of an eye-stinging, skin blistering ammoniac mist spreading over the land. The Earth opens quaking and rumbling and spewing hot caustic gas.

No one is able to remain standing. Everyone including reporters, Jimmy Disciple, Colonel Steve Golub-Singh, Mr. Tchump and all his entourage, slide slowly, almost comically down the side of the gravel bank created from burying the bus. They disappear into a gaping dark fissure under the front of the bus. There is no video or record of any of this, only the word of one survivor who tells how the house, the garage, the orange school bus and Tchump's limo all disappeared into the steaming fissure.

SIXTY-SEVEN

Grampa Joe's eyesight has been poor since childhood when he had pink eye. Sure, he hunted and fired guns with his father. But he'd be the first to tell you what a poor shot he is.

When he spies the little figure turning the corner of fourth Street and Woods Avenue carrying what he believes is his lovely nineteenth century mantle clock, his amygdala floods him with blind anger.

He mutters to himself, "Goddamned Mexican. Just look at her ... those bright crazy hippie clothes!"

His brain flashes back to a time when he hated hippies and their long hair and crazy clothes ... hippies revolting against and breaking every law, every rule of society just because they thought they were so Goddamned smart.

Grampa Joe raises the semi-automatic weapon the Sherriff issued him. Just the fact that the sheriff armed him legitimizes using it in his mind. Besides, he only means to fire warning shots ... just enough to scare some sense into that little hippie girl.

To this day he doesn't remember pulling the trigger. It seems almost impossible in hindsight that he squeezed off eight shots. But these new automatic guns ... Then, in disbelief, the sick reality hits him as he watches the little figure with the red frizzy hair jolt backward and sprawl on the sidewalk.

Only one of his bullets finds its mark. But it lodges in her pure sweet heart.

Dahlia doesn't feel any pain.

She never knew what hit her.

SIXTY-EIGHT

Three thousand miles North of Lake Pontchartrain in Ontario Canada at end of Lake Huron Mother Earth's cleavage begins. It tears apart rock and magma. The fissure rips south along the entire length of the Mississippi river where massive riverboats, barges, and gingerbread tourist paddle wheels are swallowed. Upon contact with white-hot magma, scalded water flumes skyward and forms acidic clouds. Lava slops across roads, fields, and forests. Crows caw and fly east. Mountains shudder and fall.

For seventeen hours the Earth labors violently. She screams in pain. Every creature living and crawling upon her surface struggles to survive. Many lay upon the Earth's sweaty skin crying, cowering, and covering their heads with hands or paws. Any churches still standing are packed to the choir row rafters with recently converted sinners moaning penance. As they slip into the subterranean Valley of the Shadow of Death they cry for loved ones lost and petition a deaf Lord for mercy.

When the tremors first started, radio talk show pundits blamed the first Black Woman President. Scientists were interviewed ad-nauseam and asked to explain arcane theories of polar inversion and global ion swarms. Doomsday Predictors and seers of the future ooze from the woodwork claiming propriety. Military patrols are dispatched to find Colonel Steve who many believe, by virtue of his knowledge of karma filters, might have insight into what is happening. But all they can find is his smashed chronograph watch.

A contingent of marines is dispatched to find Harold but no trace of him or Charles is ever found except for a note on Harold's desk which reads, "You people have no freaking idea what is about to happen. You just have no idea!"

SIXTY-NINE

AFTERWARD.

Albert had been wrong. Absentmindedness? How could he have forgotten to include the universal need to procreate in his "mis-mangled" calculations?

"You didn't watch. You didn't learn," Terrier said smirking.

Had Albert paid attention to the criticals it should have been obvious that Earth's pushing and grunting was not some millennium meltdown, but the natural progression of her pregnancy and labor. Had he only just backed away for one moment from his pre-conceived notions, like he was always telling others to do, he would have seen mother Earth's clenching and pushing was her going into labor. She was pushing her offspring from her sweet inner sanctum iron core. Belching flames and white-hot iron fluids should have been an unmistakable clue. Yes, she was preparing to come into her planet milk. But that milk was for her baby. For twenty-four hours Mother Earth undulated. She rolled. Gripped by the pains of labor she'd cursed mother sun – the life force from whom she herself had sprung so long ago.

A tiny milky-white head crested from Mother Earth's mountainous and mossy labia. Celestial Angels sang. Cosmic clarinets blared. Harps with gold-wound strings harmonized with booming natural stone pipe organs gouged from canyon walls. These pipes had not bellowed like this since Mother Earth herself was born. An arid desert sang with reed-blown space-wind joy announcing to all in the Universe the birth of blessed Earth's newborn baby moon … named Blue.

And the sweet little orb floated free!

SEVENTY

Today there are two moons floating above Planet Earth – two orbs beneath which Slipper and Terrier cuddle at night. Terrier is soon well enough to attend Dahlia's memorial. Brain is inconsolable. Seated in New Orleans' giant hologram plaza, the Eins and many spectators watch Dalia's death ceremony. Dahlia's ashes have been shuttled to the surface of Baby Blue Moon in a Spider11 capsule. Attendees of the ceremony solemnly watch as a drone emerges from the capsule to spread her ashes on the plateau called "Tranquility Wonder."

As the projection builds her likeness wearing her Dahlia print dress to life-like proportions, The Commissioner eulogizes, "She was a true flower ... our Dahlia. We shall always love you, Dahlia ... as Mother Earth and Baby Blue Moon love you. Goodbye, sweet flower. Goodbye."

SEVENTY-ONE

A few days after Dahlia's funeral, Terrier asks The Commissioner if he could speak with him privately for a moment.

"What's on your mind, son?" The Commissioner asks.

"Sir ... something has come up," says Terrier.

"Well, spit it out!" says The Commissioner. He seems preoccupied of late.

"Sir ... I know it would be against Interstellar law for me to do so ... but it is my intention to stay here on Earth," he says.

"Are you nuts?" asks The Commissioner.

"I want... to be with an Earthling woman whom I have fallen in love with, sir. Her name is Slipper. She has agreed to marry me," says Terrier.

"Marry you? But ... your "condition?" says The Commissioner, "You do know what I'm talking about, right? ... your operation!"

"Slipper knows about that. We've discussed it. And I have agreed to undergo T-cell gonad re-construction surgery. Apparently they've come a long way in this kind of sexual surgery here." replies Terrier.

"Oh, good Fard!" says the Commissioner, "This is crazy! You're not going to believe this, Terrier, but I was about to announce something along those lines to you and Albert and Pilot ... about my intention of remaining here on Earth to be with the human I have fallen in love with."

"Is that the woman named Bella?"

"Yes, it is."

"But what about your plans to travel to Alfa Sentori? Didn't you come all the way out here to drain Sinoid with Galaxy leaders?" asks Terrier.

"The laws are pretty clear. No one knows them better than me. If I leave Earth I will never be allowed back here," says The Commissioner.

SEVENTY-TWO

The Commissioner, Terrier, Slipper, Bella, Bear, Carlo and Laphonso watch from Bella's porch as The Beagle HU-X2 blasts off carrying Pilot and Albert back to Torikk.

Brain is in re-hab. The Hairy Colonizer will be among the first to colonize Earth's new moon. Honored for her bacterial research by the Biological Society of Louisiana, The Hairy Colonizer has been issued the first permit for breeding selected beneficial bacteria on the surface of baby, Blue Moon.

SEVENTY-THREE

When Mrs. Powers knocks on Carlo's door it swings. She peeks in asking, "Anybody home?"

Laphonso appears. He walks with the confidence of the Dog In The Manger. Laphonso is followed by Carlo, who emerges from his bedroom.

"Oh hi!" says Carlo.

"Hello Carlo," she says standing in the doorway, hands nervously rubbing each other. Carlo can see she has been crying.

"What's wrong?"

"Oh nothing ... only I found out last night my husband ... is married to me ...and to another woman,"

"Oh Christ," says Carlo.

She runs to Carlo sobbing in his arms. Her chest and shoulders heave as she holds Carlo close. Then she kisses him deeply on the mouth with salt. Laphonso presses close hoping for an ear rub.

Thank you for reading.
Please review this book. Reviews help others find
Absolutely Amazing Ebooks
and inspires us to keep providing these marvelous tales.

If you would like to be put on our email list to receive
updates on new releases, contests, and promotions, please
go to AbsolutelyAmazingEbooks.com
and sign up.

About the Author

Dale Dapkins is a 1968 psychology graduate of the University of Rochester.

He lived in Turkey for two years with the Peace Corps making a movie for the Turkish Tourism Ministry in the late sixties. After apprenticing to an Armenian Oriental Rug dealer, he became an independent antique Oriental rug expert/dealer.

His first novel *American Broccoli and Dr. Breast* was published by Nefyn and Shaw in 1988.

He won the Grand Prize in the Lorian Hemingway Short Story Competition in 1999 ... a blind read with thousands of entries from all over the world. And he won it again the following year.

He won several money prizes in Writer's Digest and other competitions.

In addition, he is a painter with several museum shows, including a one-man show at the Key West Art and Historical Society in 2006. Over twenty-four of his paintings are found in corporate collections worldwide, including eight at Zurich-Re in New York City's One Chase Manhattan Plaza.

Want More?

If you enjoyed *Blue Moon* by Dale Dapkins, you will want to browse Absolutely Amazing eBooks (AbsolutelyAmazingEbooks.com) for other great titles by this author.

We know you'll be delighted with all the great titles you find there, with more being added all the time – ebooks that are never priced higher than $3.99 ... and often much less!

ABSOLUTELY AMAZING eBOOKS

AbsolutelyAmazingEbooks.com or
AA-eBooks.com